DEADLY
WISH

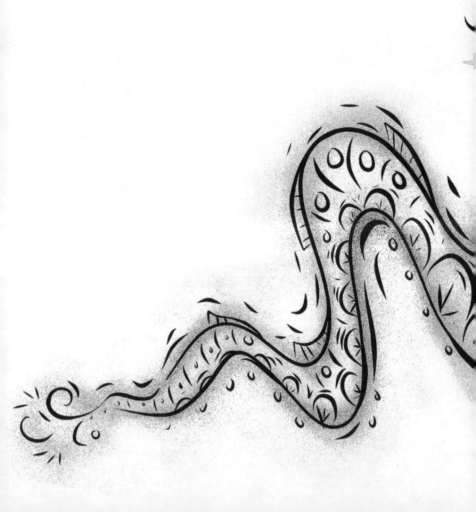

[TWEEN]

A NINJA'S JOURNEY

DEADLY WISH

SARAH L. THOMSON

BOYDS MILLS PRESS
AN IMPRINT OF HIGHLIGHTS
Honesdale, Pennsylvania

Text copyright © 2017 by Sarah L. Thomson
Ornaments copyright © 2017 by Jim Carroll

Boyds Mills Press
An Imprint of Highlights
815 Church Street
Honesdale, Pennsylvania 18431

Printed in the United States of America
ISBN: 978-1-62979-777-9 (hc)
ISBN: 978-1-62979-920-9 (e-book)

Library of Congress Control Number: 2017937880

First edition
Design by Anahid Hamparian
The text of this book is set in Bembo.
10 9 8 7 6 5 4 3 2 1

*Dedicated to
Ann and Trina—
ninja friends
extraordinaire!*

ONE

A bamboo floor can seem as long and as wide as a field of rice when you are cleaning it on your knees.

Whisking a small broom across the smooth boards, I swept dust and grit off the veranda. I was careful to keep my head bowed and my back bent, though my humble posture didn't stop Goro, my master's cook, from giving me a kick as he passed.

There was a time I would have made sure his kick never landed and broken his ankle for trying. Today I merely set down the broom and dipped a rag into the bucket beside me. Goro grunted as he disappeared around a corner of the house.

I wrung the rag half-dry. The mixture of water and vinegar made quick work of the dirty smudges from Goro's bare feet. As I rubbed, I ignored the throb of my bruised thigh where his kick had connected. I also paid no mind to the tightness in my lower back or the ache in my knees. I'd been trained for hours of swordplay, to pick locks, to escape manacles. But no one had ever warned me that cleaning a floor was such hard work.

I hung the rag over the bucket's edge and picked up the broom once more. By the time I'd swept myself into a far corner of the veranda, I heard the gate from the street swing open and shut. Footsteps approached along the curve of the garden path. I didn't look up as the newcomer paused to slip off his sandals before stepping onto the pale, gleaming boards I had just wiped clean. The door with its paper screen slid aside, and Kumawaka, a servant who had been with my master since his seafaring days, greeted the guest.

"Oh, Captain Mori. Please do enter. I hope the winds were kind to you?"

"Kumawaka, always here. It's been three years and nothing about you has changed. Your master is expecting me, I've no doubt."

I had not glimpsed our visitor's face yet, since it would be presumptuous of me to look up. But what I could hear of his voice sounded both cheerful and pleased with himself. It was the voice of a man who has a success to report. That was exactly what I had been hoping to hear.

"Oh, indeed, Captain. Please do us the honor of entering."

The screen door slid shut, cutting off the conversation from my ears.

I picked up my washrag and hurried across the garden path to hang it over the top of the gate to dry. As I did so, a shabby beggar boy, crouched in the street to poke at a beetle with a stick, looked up and caught my eye. A moment later he was pelting away as fast as he could run.

I returned to the veranda, hoisted the sloshing bucket of dirty water to my hip, and headed around the corner of the house, in the direction Goro had taken earlier.

TWO

As I paused in the kitchen doorway, one of the guard dogs came up from behind me. Hidden in the folds of my wide cloth belt, there was a sticky clump of rice. I slipped it out and let the dog lick it eagerly from my fingers.

Goro, kneeling on the cook's bamboo platform along one side of the kitchen, was setting out a tray. On it were cakes of sweet red bean paste and an elegant teapot with a milky green glaze, which had come all the way from the kingdom of Choson across the sea. Master Sakuma wanted every guest to know that, while he was no samurai, no nobleman, no courtier at the emperor's palace, he could afford the same things they had—and better, if he wanted.

Goro poured in the boiling water, and the wisps of steam rising from the pot smelled like spring. I lugged my bucket over the threshold, toward the stone sink in the corner, where a bamboo pipe let wastewater outside. Goro didn't glance at me. I slowed my steps. If my timing wasn't perfect here, my entire plan might unravel like poorly woven cloth.

The inner door slid open. Kumawaka stood there, waving his hands anxiously.

"Tea, tea, tea, is it ready? The master does not want to wait!"

I tripped. As I fell, the bucket flew from my hands, dancing across the kitchen floor to drench Kumawaka in pungent vinegar and filthy water from the waist of his indigo kimono to the white socks on his feet.

He squawked. On hands and knees on the slick dirt floor, I gasped, frozen and wide-eyed.

"You! You!" Kumawaka shrieked, holding the skirts of his dripping kimono away from his skin. "Clumsy! Careless! Useless! I will teach you *such* a lesson. Get up, stupid girl. What's your name again?"

"Raku, master," I whimpered, crawling to his feet. I tried to brush at his soggy clothing with my grubby hands.

"Don't *touch* me!" He swung a hand at me and I scuttled back. "You'll make it worse, you slimy little toad!"

Goro watched us with a dull interest. He wouldn't mind seeing me beaten, but he didn't mind seeing Kumawaka humiliated, either. His sour nature wasn't personal; he seemed to hold a grudge against the world, resenting the water that wouldn't boil fast enough, the fish that was never fresh enough, the new maid his master had taken on two months ago, and the old servant who had authority over him in name only. Goro took orders from the kitchen fire and the gods and no one else.

"Tea's brewed," he said shortly, lifting the lid of the teapot to breathe in the steam.

"I can't serve in this state!" Kumawaka wailed, dripping.

Goro shrugged. "Send the girl. Beat her later." And he turned his attention to a long white radish that needed chopping.

Kumawaka fumed for a moment and then scowled at me, still cowering penitently on the floor. "You. *Girl.*" He spat the word. "Take in the tea. Don't make the master wait or it will be worse for you later. I promise you it will be bad enough as it is!"

I bowed—more of a crouch, really, like a frightened dog—and took up the tray as Kumawaka stamped off to change his clothes, trailing dirty water as he went. Water that I would undoubtedly have to wipe up once I was done serving tea.

I hurried out with the tray, making my way through the house's central room, the one where Master Sakuma most often entertained his guests as if he were a samurai and not a humble merchant. It was empty. Good. That meant that my master had taken Captain Mori to his private study. Usually only Kumawaka was allowed to slide open the screen door to that room. Before today, I'd never been permitted even to sweep dirt off the floor mats.

If Master Sakuma and his guest were in there, it meant the captain had brought a treasure beyond price. And *that* meant the last two months of scrubbing floors and pulling weeds and enduring Goro's foul temper had been worth it.

Taking care to let my footsteps make no noise at all, I

set down my tray beside the study door. Then I crossed the room and slid open the window farthest to the left, giving me a view of the front garden. The beggar boy who'd run away earlier was back in the street; I could see him peering in over the top of the gate.

I left the second window closed, slid open the third, and watched the boy dart away once more. Then I crossed the room again, letting my footsteps sound a bit heavier this time, and knelt to slide open the study door. Picking up the tray again, I rose to my feet.

My eyes darted back and forth, taking in all I could. I would not be here long, and I needed to learn as much as possible before the tea was poured.

The study was a small room, but Sakuma had made sure that any guest would know his wealth. There was a desk set into the wall underneath a window, ink and brushes and an abacus standing ready, and a few scarlet cushions nearby. The two mats that covered the floor were new and shiny, the scroll hanging on the wall was elaborate in its calligraphy, and Master Sakuma, kneeling with Captain Mori, had on a black kimono that glittered with embroidery and moved with the heavy grace of the finest silk from the Ming Empire.

He frowned just a little on seeing me; of course he had expected Kumawaka. But he didn't want to admit in front of a guest that anything about his household came as a surprise. So he merely went on talking over my head as I knelt again to pour the steaming tea into small cups of gleaming green porcelain.

"Yes, Ryujin was gracious to our voyage, no doubt," the captain said, taking his cup from my hand without glancing at me.

"I will visit the old water dragon's shrine," Sakuma answered. "And the jade pendant you found will make an excellent gift for the youngest Takeda boy. He's just taken a wife. Perhaps you hadn't heard? Of course I want to pay my respects."

"Who did his father find to marry that worm?" the captain asked, amused. "I'm surprised he was able to lift his nose out of his wine cup long enough to finish the cere-mony."

"A girl from a mountain province, or so I've been told. Niece to some warlord or other. Pretty enough, but—what was that?"

That was what I had been listening for.

The dogs were barking frantically outside. Shouts from the garden and a bellow of surprise from the kitchen were followed by Goro's furious cry: "Thieves! Thieves!"

Sakuma rose to his feet in alarm, and Captain Mori got up as well, laying a hand on the hilt of his longer sword.

I dashed to the door, teapot swinging from my hand, to see two black-clad figures, scarves over their faces, pelt from the kitchen into the central room. I fell back into the study with a startled squeak, like a mouse that had been stepped on, and Captain Mori pushed past me, his sword now out of its sheath. The two thieves took one look at him and fled. He followed.

"Guards! Where are my guards!" Master Sakuma called out, panic in his voice. He was not a ship captain or a samurai; he had no swords at his belt.

"Master! The window!" I shrieked.

Just after I spoke, a heavy club smashed through the thin wooden slats and the frail rice paper of the window over the desk. Another black-clad figure was climbing in. Master Sakuma made a quick, darting movement toward the desk. His hand reached out before he snatched it back and jumped away. Rich, plump, and lazy, fond of his bed and his meals, he was no match for a wiry young thief holding a knife that flashed in the sun.

I flung the teapot as hard as I could.

Pale amber tea splattered the tatami mats, the desk, and my master. The teapot caught the intruder square in the face, so that he cried out and fell backward through the window.

The sounds of shouting men and running footsteps told us that the guards outside were approaching at last. The thief took to his heels, leaving behind a damp room, a ruined window, a broken teapot, a very relieved merchant, and a maidservant who had just saved the day.

Chujiro and Taro, the two guards, claimed that there had been at least a dozen thieves. Even allowing for natural exaggeration—for what guard wants to admit that a few ragtag thieves had burst into the house and been within a few feet of his master?—six or eight of the criminals must have been working together. On some signal, Taro said, they'd all climbed the hedges and raced for the house, hoping that at least one or two would make it inside.

A signal, perhaps, like a rag over a gate, or two

windows open and one shut.

Master Sakuma told his guards at length what he thought of men who left their employer to be defended by a guest and a skinny little scrap of a servant girl. Captain Mori was loaded down with gifts and gratitude, and I was promised a new kimono and an extra bowl of black rice that evening—plus being spared from the beating Kumawaka had promised me. Master Sakuma even magnanimously forgave me for breaking his most valuable teapot.

Not a bad day, I thought, as I lay beside the kitchen stove that night, listening to Goro's breathing settle down into steady snoring.

Goro had tried to fight off the thieves himself, armed with no more than a ladle, and earned a noticeable bump over one eyebrow for his trouble. Master Sakuma had given him an extra cup of rice wine that evening, and when Goro's back was turned, I had added something to make sure that his snores would continue unabated until dawn.

Kumawaka, fortunately, considered himself too grand to sleep in the kitchen; he had his own little cubbyhole of a room where he laid out his mattress and kept his belongings. I did not have to concern myself with him tonight.

I sat up cautiously, waited to be sure Goro had not stirred, and crawled to the woodpile in the corner. Working slowly and silently, I shifted most of the logs and tugged out something I'd hidden underneath them a few days earlier.

It only took a moment to slip off the ragged, undyed kimono that had helped turn me into the servant girl Raku and leave it in a heap on the floor. I drew on the clothing I had taken from the woodpile—trousers, a short jacket, a long sash to wrap around my waist, a hood to hold my hair back, all of it dyed a blue that was very nearly black. I touched the warm stones of the stove and rubbed soot over my hands and face. Now there was nothing about me that would stand out in the night. The shadows would welcome me as one of their own.

I picked up the knife that had been hidden under the clothes and slid it into a sheath along my forearm. Then I tied my sandals together and slung them over my shoulder.

One of Raku's jobs had been to see to it that the doors of Master Sakuma's household were well oiled and free of dirt or grit, so that they would not stick or scrape. I had always been most conscientious about that chore. The keenest ear would not have heard a sound as I slipped out of the kitchen and entered the central room.

The windows were shuttered. I did not even have the dim glow of a banked stove to help me. This I would have to do by memory. I kept to the edges of the room, where the bamboo floors had been less used and weren't as likely to groan or squeak. On each step I eased my bare foot down, rolling my weight from the outer edge to the inner. I could feel every woven strand in the smooth mats under my feet as I counted my strides. Six along the wall that the central room shared with the kitchen. Turn the corner. Eight more and there was the door to Master Sakuma's private study.

This time I had no need to kneel before entering.

Once inside, I shut the door behind me and stood still. It was really the kind of job I needed a dark lantern for, but that would have been too much to smuggle into the house and keep hidden from Goro's watchful eye. The clothes and the knife had been difficult enough.

I would have to complete this task without using my sight. I closed my eyes so that I would not distract myself by straining to see. My other senses opened up like night-blooming flowers. Hearing sharpened. My sense of smell heightened. My skin tingled with eagerness to touch.

I could hear my own breath in my nostrils, my pulse beating against my temples and in my throat. I shifted my awareness outside my own skin and heard leaves brush against the wooden shutters, someone singing a cheerful drinking song, unsteady footsteps scuffling over the road. I heard heavy breathing coming from the room next door, where Master Sakuma slept. Through the thin rice paper of the door, I smelled the sweat on his skin, garlic and pepper and wine on his breath.

It was a pity I had not managed to drug his drink as well, but Goro had left me no chance. The rhythm of the merchant's breath, steady but not too steady, told me he was genuinely asleep, though not deeply. Any noise could stir him into wakefulness.

I'd have to make no noise, then.

I let the room take shape in my memory. I had only seen it once, but that one time had been enough. I stood without moving until the vision was clear in front of my closed eyes, and then gently slid one bare foot along the floor.

The study was long enough for two mats laid side by side. The sole of my foot found the crack between them, and I followed it. After five steps I stopped, then inched forward until the desk in its alcove bumped against my shin.

I eased myself down so that I was kneeling before it, just as Master Sakuma must every day, calculating his accounts or checking lists of cargo.

My right fingers spread out to brush the mat. Earlier today, Master Sakuma had leaped toward his desk, stretching out his hand. If I could find the spot he had been reaching for . . .

There. I felt it. The edge of the mat was frayed. I took hold of the worn spot and slowly pulled the woven straw back, exposing the bare floor beneath.

Sakuma snorted in the next room. Quilts rustled and the cotton inside the mattress sighed as he turned over. I held myself motionless as a rock in a rainstorm, letting the sounds of his restlessness wash over me, until he settled into stillness once again.

I rubbed my fingertips together and breathed softly on them, giving them the extra sensitivity of warmth, then began probing gently at the floor.

When a thief had burst into his home, Sakuma's first move had been toward this place. Toward the window, toward the man with the knife, toward danger. And he was not a man who loved danger. That told me there was something precious here, something he loved almost as much as he loved his own skin.

All I had to do was find it. In darkness and silence. Before anyone could wake and discover that their meek and cringing servant girl was something else entirely.

Each bamboo board was sleek and smooth under my touch. No hint, no clue of anything unusual or out of place—until the fourth board, the one that was raised just slightly higher than its neighbors.

The difference was too small for the eye to catch. But my fingertips had felt it. Now, there must be a lock or a lever somewhere—yes. Simple. When I pressed down on one end of the board, the other sprang into my waiting hand.

I did not reach at once into the hole I had just uncovered. Instead, I slid my knife out of its sheath and used it to probe the cavity and to locate the three spikes that would have lacerated an eager and careless hand.

Avoiding the spikes, I groped in the hole and felt a soft, heavy bag of quilted silk, bundled with cord, of a size to fit easily in one hand. I plucked it out and untied the drawstrings, reaching inside to feel a tightly furled scroll, a string of coins, and several small, rough stones. Uncut jewels, I guessed. I slid one out, weighed it in my hand, and then tucked it into my mouth, securing it between my gum and upper lip.

Then I retied the bag, careful to use the same knots as before, and stowed it in a helpful pocket inside my jacket. After replacing the board and the mat, I rose to my feet and climbed onto the desk, moving slowly to hush any creaks from wood unaccustomed to such weight.

Once I'd slid the remains of the window screen

gently to one side, all that lay between me and the night was a wooden shutter. I put an ear against it and held my breath to listen.

The loudest sound was my own heartbeat, but I focused my hearing beyond that, beyond Sakuma's grunts and sighs, out to what was happening in the garden.

Wind. Grasses and the long leaves of bamboo rubbing together. Cicadas shrilling. Footsteps across the earth, the soft sigh made by the woven soles of old sandals. It was Taro. I could tell by the slight hesitation in every other step as his stiff knee took his weight. Wounded in some long-ago battle, the old veteran had been glad to find a job as a guard for a rich merchant who kept a good table.

There came a sigh, and I heard Taro's hands rubbing together, the dry skin rasping. Even in late spring, the nights could still be chilly. Then his footsteps went on.

I let my breath out slowly and counted ten heartbeats after the last footfalls had faded away before I lifted the latch on the shutter and slid it open. With my sandals still over my shoulder, I slipped to the ground, reaching up to close the shutter after me. It was a shame that I could not fasten the latch on the inside, to leave no trace at all of my passing. But from the outside, no one would see the difference.

I did not have to worry about Taro returning soon. I'd spent more than one night crouched silently at a window, and one stretched flat on a rooftop, watching the two guards and learning their habits. Taro spent most of his time by the kitchen door; Chujiro rarely stirred from the front of the house. They walked through the garden now and again, but for the most part they relied on the dogs.

The dogs, that is, who were at that moment racing toward me in the dark.

THREE

I could hear the soft, rapid footfalls of the two dogs on the earth. "Easy, now, easy," I whispered, slipping my hand into my belt.

There were the bits of sea urchin, wrapped in rice to keep them safe, that I had filched from dinner. (It had been Goro's dinner, and not mine, of course. Goro was not a man to waste fresh fish on a servant girl's dinner, even a servant girl who'd saved her master's property, and maybe his life, by her aim with a teapot.)

I dared not raise my voice; Taro and Chujiro might have been lazy, but they were by no means stupid. If I or the dogs made noise, they'd investigate. I'd have to hope that my own scent, and that of the food, would reassure the animals.

I felt two cold, wet noses nuzzling eagerly at my out-stretched hands, two warm tongues licking. I stroked soft ears and rubbed furry necks. The dogs didn't have names; they were not pets. But I called them Brown and Black, and I'd taken care to make good friends with them. In their minds I was no stranger, no threat, and no reason to bark.

I flung another handful of food on the ground and left the dogs nosing the dirt as I crossed the garden.

I didn't run; there was no need and not enough light, either. I stayed on the grass, away from the gravel of the path, and soon I was picking my way, still barefoot, through rows of cucumbers and radishes. At the end of the garden was the hedge, and in the hedge was the hole I'd made behind the shelter of an exceptionally leafy burdock plant. Each time Goro sent me to weed or water or pick what he needed, I'd scrape away a handful or two of dirt or break off twigs that would block my path. Now I paused to tie my sandals on before I slid headfirst into the hollow I'd made between the bare roots and the prickly branches. Careful not to crush the precious package inside my jacket, I wriggled my way out of Master Sakuma's household.

Slowly, in no hurry, I stood to my full height, brushed bits of dirt and bark off my jacket, and breathed out. For the first time that night, I relaxed enough to notice the weather—the damp air, the clouds that covered the moon and deepened the darkness, the mist that brushed the skin on my face with little pinpricks of chill and carried with it a hint of salt from the sea.

It was too dark to run, so I jogged easily down the street. There was no great need for haste. It was only the hour of the rat, and half the night was still to pass before dawn broke and Master Sakuma would wake to learn that his servant girl and his secret treasure were both missing.

I felt the last traces of Raku the drudge slip away,

falling from me like scraps of a snake's discarded skin. My shoulders shook off their furtive hunch; my gaze lifted from the packed dirt of the road to scan the lanes and buildings ahead of me. I had been Raku for two months, ever since Sakuma's former servant girl had been given a surprising gift of money by a stranger in the marketplace and told to go back to her village and buy herself a husband. It felt good to move like myself once more.

I crossed the city's wide main avenue, which began at the harbor and ran all the way up the city's highest hill. Along it were the mansions of the city's rich and powerful. The higher on the hill their mansions stood, the richer the families were. Highest of all, of course, were the Takedas. This was their city. They'd rule the tides if they could.

But as if to remind them that they could not, on the very top of the hill was the shrine to the dragon god Ryujin. He was the one who sent the tides in and out twice each day. Even here, at a distance from the water, my ear could still catch the soft growl and sigh of waves advancing and retreating against the coarse pebbles of the shore.

A little farther, I reached an arched bridge over the river that, like a slow-moving snake, coiled lazily among houses and streets. Inside my mind I consulted the map of the city opening up like a long scroll, and I skirted the pleasure district, the only place where people were likely to be stirring. From there I could hear scraps of laughter and broken song. Dressed as I was, I'd have drawn too much attention from musicians and actors, courtesans and customers, if I'd ventured into their space.

I jogged down a street of simple shops, their goods

taken in, their shutters closed for the night. Even here, I had to be careful. There were voices around a corner up ahead. I slowed and stopped, listening to a high-pitched giggle and a deeper answer. A man and a woman, coming this way, carrying light to spoil my friendly darkness.

I backed into a side street just before the pair turned the corner. He wore the two swords of a samurai and had a lantern in his hand, as well as a round straw hat pulled low over his face. No warrior wanted to be recognized on his way to or from the pleasure district, especially with such a woman clinging to his arm as she wobbled a bit on her high wooden clogs.

If her elaborate kimono and her pretty face did not announce that she was a courtesan, her hair, gathered up to expose the slender nape of her neck, made it perfectly clear. And she was a particularly brazen one, to be out on the street with a male companion.

I had guessed the two of them would continue along the wider street. To my dismay, however, they turned down the same lane I had chosen for concealment. I'd knelt against a hedge, where my dark clothes and blackened face should have turned me into nothing but another nighttime shadow. But a shadow cannot defeat light.

The woman was singing now, her voice blurred by wine; the man was laughing; they were passing within ten feet of me. The pool of light cast by the samurai's lantern bobbed a few inches from my left knee, and I silently slid my knife from its sheath. A knife against two swords was no fair fight, but add surprise to that knife and the odds came considerably closer to even.

Luckily, I did not need to try those odds. The couple continued on their unsteady way and turned into a narrow alley between two houses. I waited a moment to be sure that they were truly gone before I sheathed my knife and got to my feet.

Carefully, I checked my mental map of the city. It wasn't easy to find the way among winding streets and alleys, even in broad daylight; I had to be sure I didn't take a wrong turn.

This street held craftsmen's homes: cobblers and potters, a basket weaver, a man who made clogs and another who sold combs. One building showed the dim light of an oil lamp through a screen, with a shadow cast on the rice paper. Someone was working late. The hunched figure behind the screen rose and stretched, as if to ease an aching back.

I turned away. Time to keep moving. As I did so, I heard a soft sound behind me, something between a pop and a crunch.

The sound of a paper screen breaking. I spun around.

The light from the house I had noticed earlier was brighter now, because two or three panels of the paper screen had been broken. And coming toward me, outlined against that light, was a shape on two legs—but not a human shape.

Oh, no. Not here, not now . . .

My knife was in my hand as I backed up carefully, putting distance between myself and the thing approaching me.

The creature should have been awkward, balanced on

two legs, but it was not. Lithe and muscled, as tall as my shoulder, it stalked toward me, lamplight brushing soft gray fur. It let out a soft, hungry meow.

Two tails waved, helping the thing keep its balance. Its ears were flattened, its whiskers swept back; the green-gold eyes were narrow and hungry. A double-tailed cat, a neko-mata.

I'd been pleased to have finished my mission, to be out in the night, to be done acting like a timid and stupid servant girl to fool stupider men. And so I'd gotten careless. How could I have forgotten to be on my guard at every moment? Had I let myself believe that there was nothing in this darkened city more dangerous than I was?

Careless. I'd pay for that carelessness now.

The neko-mata faced me and the corners of its mouth pulled back in a snarl. Its teeth were half the length of my longest finger.

"Mine," it whined, an unnatural sound, human words forced out of an animal's throat. "Mine, mine . . ."

Its back legs flexed as it drew itself together to leap.

A cat will stalk a mouse for long minutes before it finally closes in for the kill. But the last dash and pounce happen as quickly as fire moving from twig to twig. I threw myself facedown just as the neko-mata jumped, and it passed over me, its back claws brushing my hood. Rolling, I came up in a crouch to see the cat land, whirl, and leap again, all in a single movement.

The beast was too fast. I could not dodge again. I barely had time to throw both hands out—one gripping the knife, one ready to grab—and fling myself backward as it hit. We tumbled across the dirt; the neko-mata was on top. Had it somehow grown bigger in the air?

Its front claws jabbed into my forearms, which I was using to keep the thing away from my throat. The back legs were coming up, ready to disembowel me. Neko-mata always craved human flesh. This one would be happy to feast on my intestines—after it had gotten what it had attacked me for.

I got my knee up and kicked hard, connecting with the creature's rib cage. It yowled. Other cats answered from behind hedges and fences and shutters, along rooftops and alleys, and I realized that we had an audience. Had every feline in the city come to watch me die?

Well, if they had, they were going to be disappointed.

My kick threw the neko-mata off. It flopped gracelessly on its back, caught off balance for a moment, and I leaped upon it.

I avoided the head, with the snarling mouth and needle-sharp teeth. I ducked away from the claws, which slashed the air beside my face, snagging a hank of hair. I took aim at the tails.

A double-tailed cat was a thing of magic and menace. What would it be if it had no tails at all?

I sliced. Warm blood sprayed. The neko-mata shrieked. And it shrank under my hands like a doll that had lost its stuffing, so that two seconds later an ordinary house cat raced tailless down the street, yowling in anguish. The watching cats screeched their dismay.

More lights were beginning to glimmer behind paper screens as I rose, checking with my tongue to be sure that the jewel I'd taken from Master Sakuma's pouch was still in place inside my mouth. It was. Someone not far to my left slid a shutter open. Voices rose.

"What is it?"

"Fire?"

"Thieves?"

"Is it bandits?"

I could not be found here in my dark clothing and soot-smeared face, splattered with blood. I ran for a house that was still dark, jumped, and in a moment was on the low, thatched roof. Several cats were ranged along the ridgepole above my head. I looked up, drew back my lips to show my teeth, and hissed; they scattered in panic.

I followed their example. It was not hard to move from roof to roof, hurdling the gaps between houses. I jumped over an alley and glanced down to catch the pale face of the courtesan I had seen earlier lifting toward me as I flew through the air over her head. Beside her in the lantern light, lying facedown, was the body of the samurai, which she had been stripping of weapons and valuables.

I followed the rooftops for as long as I could, easily outpacing the clamor and confusion behind me. When at last I was forced to jump down, I found myself in a street of simple but prosperous homes—hedges neatly trimmed, roofs freshly thatched, small gardens with beds of moss and carefully spaced boulders under artistically pruned trees. It was too dark to see any of this at the moment, but that didn't matter. I knew what was there.

I walked up to one such garden, knocked at the gate,

spoke briefly to the man who had been waiting, and was allowed inside.

Entering the house, I strode along the earthen passage that ran straight from the front door to the back. To my right was the raised platform where the owners of the dwelling lived and slept; I heard someone there sigh irritably and turn over. But the sleepers were used to midnight comings and goings, and no one opened an eye or lifted a head. They were paid well not to.

Just before I would have stepped out the back door, I paused, laid my hand on a panel of the left-hand wall, and pushed. It swung silently inward, and I stepped into the dark hole that had been revealed.

FOUR

The passageway I'd entered was pitch-black, but I didn't need light. I counted twenty-five paces, reached out to slide another door open, and entered a hallway lined with mats and lit by the warm glow of an oil lamp. Any watchers in the street would have seen me enter a house and not leave again; they'd have no way of knowing that I was now in a different building altogether.

A boy who had been kneeling beside the door rose to his feet. He was about my own age, young enough to be gangly still, with an indigo jacket that was too short for his arms. Over his left cheekbone was a puffy, red swelling, starting to bruise, where I had hit him with a teapot when he tried to climb into Master Sakuma's house.

He nodded, not surprised to see me, but satisfied. My presence marked a mission completed. "You have it?" he asked.

I gave him an irritated look. He laughed. "I didn't ask. Of course you have it."

"Is he in his room, Jinnai?" I asked, careful not to let the pebble hidden in my mouth alter my speech.

Jinnai nodded. "He is. Waiting for you. He expected you a bit sooner." I saw his gaze flicker down to the ripped sleeve of my jacket, but my dark clothes concealed the worst of the neko-mata's blood. At any rate, Jinnai would never have been rude enough to ask about the details of my assignment if I did not volunteer them.

"I had something to take care of" was all I said. Brushing past him, I made my way down the hall.

"You have good aim!" he called after me.

"You knew that when you climbed in the window. You should have ducked," I answered without looking back.

When I got to a door, I paused and raised my voice a little. "Master Ishikawa? I've returned."

"Enter," came the command.

I did so.

Master Ishikawa's room was so simple it looked almost bare. It was odd that, at the same time, it made Master Sakuma's private study look like a peasant's hut.

The screen along one side of the room, where just a few strokes of black and gray ink conjured an island out of a misty bay, had been done by Sesshu. A small brazier stood on three legs, a few coals smoldering in it to take any night-time chill out of the air. Master Ishikawa knelt near it, his back to the door, counting jewels that he'd spread across his desk. Occasionally he held one up to the oil lamp so that the blood red of a ruby or the tawny smoke of a chunk of amber seemed to gather the light and give it back with a richer, more opulent glow.

Most men would not kneel with their backs to the door, counting riches that could buy a castle complete with the warlord inside it. Most men would post guards or hire soldiers or at least lock the door.

Master Ishikawa was not most men.

I closed the door behind me and knelt, pressing my forehead into the mats and breathing in their fresh, grassy scent, feeling the pressure of the jewel inside my lip. The stone was too small to leave a visible lump, but it felt as if I were trying to hide an unshelled walnut.

Every thief who worked for Ishikawa Goemon had heard what happened to the rare and rash employee who had stolen from the master. And so no one ever stole from him. Which had led me to wonder if the stories were true, or merely convenient.

This might be the mission where I found out.

"Kata," Master Ishikawa said, laying an emerald delicately down on his desk and turning to me with a smile. "So pleasant to have you home again. Show me, please." He held out a hand. I straightened up, reached into my pocket, slipped out the silk bag, and handed it to my employer. Then I waited to see if he would tell me to go.

He did not, and I carefully kept all trace of pleasure from my face. He had no idea that the bag I'd given him did not contain all of Sakuma's jewels. Moreover, he was going to let me see exactly what I had stolen. Not all of Master Ishikawa's thieves got that privilege.

I had spent two years working for Master Ishikawa, seeking him out not long after I'd first arrived in the Takedas' city. He'd been impressed that I'd managed to locate his home, make my way inside it, and leave two of his bodyguards helpless on the ground. Instead of killing me for my presumption, he'd offered me a job.

I'd proved valuable.

Sometimes I knew what I was stealing or why I was sent to make my way into a samurai's mansion or report on a courtier's movements. Sometimes I only knew that a mysterious parcel or a bit of information was something my master needed.

Of course, I would never pester Master Ishikawa for information that he did not offer. But it was always satisfying to know why I was doing the work I did—in this case, what that greedy fool Sakuma had that was so valuable I'd spent weeks as the maidservant Raku, scrubbing floors and vegetables and waiting for Captain Mori to arrive.

Master Ishikawa untied the drawstrings that held the bag closed. He glanced inside and slipped out the scroll.

Careful to keep the surprise off my face, I watched. I knew there were other things of value in that bag; why did he seem so interested in a scrap of rice paper?

Ishikawa brushed the jewels on his desk aside as if they were nothing compared to what he now held. He smoothed the scroll flat.

It was not a priceless piece of calligraphy or a famous painting. The surface of the paper was covered with faint, scribbly lines and tiny notations. An irregular shape, like a crescent moon scrawled with a quick and careless brush, took up most of the center. Wavelike blue lines crisscrossed the background.

Master Ishikawa glanced up at my baffled face.

"You've never seen anything like this?"

I shook my head.

"No. I don't imagine you have. It's a map, child."

My forehead wrinkled. A map? I knew what maps looked like. Where were the cities, the roads, the castles?

Master Ishikawa smiled. "A map of the ocean. A map of the other lands. The territory of the Ming emperor, that's here. Choson over here. The Ryukyu kingdom. The islands to the south where spices grow. You see?"

I didn't see. A map of . . . the ocean? He might as well have said a map of the sky. How could restless water be mapped? And why would anyone want to?

Then I felt my eyes widen. A map of what lay *across* the ocean? A map of the lands over the sea?

Since I'd arrived in this city, I'd seen ships dock, carrying goods from distant kingdoms and empires. I'd watched men in the street who spoke with strange accents and wore foreign robes. Even so, I'd vaguely imagined the places that they came from swirling like clouds on the horizon, swallowing up travelers foolhardy enough to venture far from shore.

Now I'd stolen a map of these distant realms, as if they were no more outlandish than the domain of the warlord next door? I tried to get another glimpse, but Master Ishikawa was rolling the scroll back up, looking satisfied and, oddly, a bit regretful at the same time.

"You can't imagine what a ship captain will pay for a map like this. Well done, Kata. You are a valuable agent, indeed. In a way, it's a pity that the jewels I was offered for you were even more valuable."

Someone dropped down from the ceiling, landed just behind me, and seized me around the throat.

I'd allowed myself to believe that I was useful to my master, useful enough to let down my guard in his presence. I'd been weak enough to feel that, after a long mission, I'd come home.

I'd been a fool, in short. And now a rock-hard arm was tightening around my neck. Black and purple spots were starting to blot out my vision.

I gripped the arm and the shoulder connected to it, dropped to one knee, and sent my attacker flying over my head, nearly into Master Ishikawa's lap. He moved deftly aside, and she rolled and was up again only seconds after she had hit the ground. I recognized the face, teeth bared in a snarl like an angry dog's.

Fuku? Why had a ninja from my past dropped out of nowhere—no, out of a trapdoor I'd had no idea existed— to attack me?

Why was for later. Escape was for now.

But the door opened to reveal two more armed girls, and another was emerging from behind the screen in the corner, and Master Ishikawa laid a gentle and protective hand over the scroll on his desk, that mild and regretful look still on his face, as I dove to one side to avoid Fuku's next charge. They were all on me before I could rise—a knee in my back, a hand gripping my hair, a heavy weight across my legs, a foot stamping down hard on my right wrist.

I caught a glimpse of Jinnai's shocked face in the doorway before Fuku's fist, heavy with the small iron weight she had gripped in it, smashed down hard on the side of my head. The uncut jewel inside my mouth burst out and rolled across the floor as darkness fell heavily over me.

* * *

I woke inside a cage.

It took some time for me to realize it. At first, all I knew was that I was lying curled up on my side somewhere dark and hot. The arm that I lay on had gone numb. And I ached all over, particularly my head.

I tried to touch the painful, throbbing lump on my temple, and that's how I discovered my hands were bound behind me. My ankles were tied together as well, and a gag had been shoved into my mouth.

I'd gotten out of bonds like this before. The first step was to get my hands in front of me. It would be more difficult with one arm asleep, but not impossible. I arched my shoulders and began to slide my hands down the curve of my back, but stopped at once. The cord about my wrists had also been looped around my throat. It was slack enough to give me no trouble as long as my hands stayed where they were, in the small of my back. But any struggle to get free meant I'd lose the chance to breathe.

A ninja out of legend would have turned herself into smoke and slipped out of her bonds, leaving the knots untouched behind her. Since I was not a legend, I painfully and cautiously wriggled to my other side, to let the blood flow back into my cramped arm. Then I lay still and tried to use my eyes and ears to figure out where I was.

The answer was: on the bottom of a bamboo cage, perhaps three feet square, covered by thick, rough cloth. Enough light filtered through the coarse weave to let me know that the sun had risen outside.

The cage, with me in it, was moving. I was rocked and bumped and jolted, motion that, combined with the throb in my head, was making me sick to my stomach. I could hear the creak and clunk of wooden wheels and the plodding footsteps and occasional snort of oxen.

So now I knew where I was—on a cart.

I could guess where I was going.

I breathed slowly and deeply through my nose, trying to stifle the urge to throw up, which would only make everything worse. Cautiously I wiggled my shoulders, flexed my ankles, tensed and relaxed the muscles of my legs and neck and back. It was all I could do to ensure that, when I reached my destination, I would be capable of movement.

And I waited.

After a while, the cart stopped. My cage was lifted. Swaying, I was carried for a distance and then dropped onto a packed dirt floor.

The cover was pulled off.

I sat up with care, blinking. I was in what looked like, and smelled like, a barn. No animals were here now, though. I recognized one of the girls who had carried me— Tomiko. The other three were strangers to me. None of the four looked my way.

Fuku had not lowered herself to the servant's task of carrying a bamboo cage. She entered the barn now and came to crouch by the bars, peering between them to be sure her prisoner was still alive. Then she nodded and got up without a word, gesturing to the others to follow her.

So Fuku was in charge of this mission. She must be pleased about that. Indeed, I could tell that she was; I had not grown up alongside this girl without being able to read her expression perfectly well. I'd learned to stay alert for the foot that might trip me, the handful of dirt slipped into my bowl of millet porridge, the needle tucked into her collar that might be slipped out to jab me during a sparring match.

Now excitement was bubbling just below the surface of the face she was trying hard to keep calm and professional. Vanity had always been one of Fuku's weaknesses. It was something to keep in mind.

The five ninjas filed out, shutting the door behind them and leaving me alone in the almost darkness.

Time passed.

When the door slid open again, it was Tomiko who entered, with another girl I did not know at her side. She carried a bowl of rice with vegetables and another of water, which she set beside the cage as she knelt to my level.

"Kata? If you don't try to kill me, I'll untie your hands so you can eat."

I hesitated, and then twisted cautiously around so that my bound hands were near the bars. Tomiko reached in and hastily slashed the cords that bound me, pulling back quickly enough that, slow and stiff as I was, I had no chance to seize her hand or her knife.

Clumsily I worked the cords off my wrists and from around my neck, pulled the gag out of my mouth, and reached through the bars for the water. I sipped it carefully. Coolness slid down my throat and the remaining nausea eased out of my stomach. New strength flowed through my veins. Tomiko and her companion had left by the time the bowl was empty.

I freed my feet and got hold of the bowl of food, cold but welcome. I shoveled the meal down greedily and then patted the pockets of my jacket to see what had been left to me. No weapons, of course. Ninjas trained as my captors had been would not have missed anything I might have used to defend myself.

But my hands and feet were still deadly enough, if I could get them ready for use. I began to work in earnest on loosening my cramped shoulders and rigid back.

Before I had made much progress, the door to the barn slid open again. A small upright figure stood outlined against the light.

The one I had been expecting.

Madame Chiyome.

FIVE

Nothing about her had changed in the two years since I had left her school. She still held herself perfectly straight, yet not at all stiff. Her hair, white and gray, was gathered loosely at the back of her neck. Her kimono was gray, too, sober in design, rich in material. The heavy silk flowed like water about her, beginning to move a moment after she took her first step, continuing to swirl a moment after she came to a stop by my cage. Her eyes were alert and pitiless as she studied me, crouched behind bars.

In the past two years, I'd thought, more than once, that Master Ishikawa had taken me on because he could see that I was not afraid of him. Perhaps that had intrigued and impressed him. Very few people could meet the most notorious thief in all the coastal provinces without quailing.

Master Ishikawa did not know that I'd spent twelve years of my life in a school run by a mistress who made him look like a kindly grandfather. Who could fear the worm once she'd faced the dragon?

Fuku had followed Madame into the barn. Madame gave me another careful, narrow-eyed look, as if I were a horse she was thinking of buying, and she had no intention of being cheated. Then she nodded once to Fuku, who bowed and departed.

That girl had improved in self-discipline since I'd left Madame's school. Something else to keep in mind.

"You have a decision to make," Madame Chiyome said.

I did? I was a prisoner in a cage. Prisoners did not usually get to make decisions.

"My client will be here to speak with you soon," Madame went on. In the warm, stuffy dark of the barn, her voice had an odd quality, so clear and calm I felt as if I should be able to see by it, as if she'd lit a paper lantern with her words.

I'd known that Madame would not be taking me back to the school where I had grown up under her sharp eye. I had no place there anymore. Was she going to return me to the man she'd sold me to? I'd escaped from his castle and his service the very night she'd taken his string of gold coins into her hands.

"You have something in your possession that belongs to her," Madame went on.

Madame's client was not the warlord I'd briefly belonged to, then. I felt coldness gather at the base of my throat and around my heart.

"You can return her possession freely, or you will be killed. That is your choice to make."

It wasn't much of a choice.

"It's Saiko," I said, my voice a husky rasp, my mouth still

sore from the gag. "Saiko is your client."

I didn't need to make it into a question. Madame didn't treat it as such. From her face, you would not know that I'd spoken.

"I am telling you this now so that you can think over what you will do," she continued. "And I will add one more thing for you to keep in mind. This is simply a mission for me. For my client it is more than that. She is not one to accept being robbed of what she feels should be hers. If you choose death, it will not come quickly."

She turned, her kimono swirling like a whirlpool. Fuku was there to slide the barn door open and to close it after her.

Rubbing my fingers together to warm and loosen them, I slipped a hand inside my jacket to untie the cords that held a pocket shut. Inside the pocket was the object Saiko believed I had stolen from her.

Carefully, I drew it out and held it cradled in my hands.

A pearl encircled by a band of gold the width of a thin willow twig, it nearly glowed in the dimness, even pulsing a little as if with its own eerie heartbeat. Whoever had searched me while I'd been unconscious had not taken this. They'd only been looking for weapons; perhaps they had missed it. Or, more likely, Saiko had given orders that anything valuable in my possession should not be touched. As far as she was concerned, the fewer people who knew the pearl existed, the better.

The little white orb looked simple enough, valuable perhaps, but nowhere near worth the heap of jewels I'd glimpsed on Master Ishikawa's table. Nowhere near worth the trouble of kidnapping me and dumping me at Saiko's feet.

But of course the pearl wasn't what Saiko wanted, not really.

What she wanted was the demon's soul inside it.

I rolled the jewel lightly between my fingertips, feeling the cool smoothness of the pearl, the slick softness of the gold. Did I imagine a faint, deep chuckle, like stone grinding on stone, almost too distant to hear?

Hurriedly, I stowed the pearl away in my pocket once more, tying the cords tight.

I'd been the guardian of the pearl for two years now, ever since Saiko's little brother had thrust it into my hand, the silk-white surface of the jewel warm with his own blood. In that time, I'd made four wishes, calling on the power of the demon trapped inside.

Each wish had brought that demon a step closer to freedom.

Since I'd escaped from the warlord who had owned me—who happened to be Saiko's uncle—I'd never made a wish. I'd kept the pearl safe, and slowly its tendency to call forth ghosts and demons wherever I went had died down. Oh, now and then something was stirred to wakefulness and hunger by the presence of the demon in my pocket—a kappa lurking in the shallow water beneath a bridge, a ghost moaning from a well, the neko-mata last night. But those stirrings were rare, and becoming rarer. I'd thought I had the demon in check.

There were two wishes left, or perhaps one. And once they were gone, the demon would have its freedom.

It would also have the soul of the last person to make a wish.

I'd heard the demon in my mind. I'd seen the forms that it could take. And I had no wish at all to set it loose upon the world or to hand it over to Kashihara Saiko.

For a time we'd been . . . certainly not friends. Allies, perhaps. At least twice she'd saved my life. I'd come fairly close to trusting her.

That had been a mistake. But not as serious a mistake as underestimating her.

Saiko had depths to her that made Madame look shallow. Whatever happened, I could not risk letting her get her hands on this pearl.

I could spend a fifth wish. I could free myself from this cage. But if I did that, there was a good possibility I would free myself from my soul as well.

So I made no wish. I had another ploy to try first. It had already been set in motion—at least I hoped so. To see if it would work, all I had to do was wait.

❧ ❧ ❧

I spent the next day in the cage and was fed twice more. Another night fell, and Saiko did not arrive. Apparently I was being given time to make my choice.

Before the cracks in the barn walls began to brighten with daylight for a second time, someone pushed the door open again, just enough for a slim body to slip through. Footsteps, very nearly silent, padded toward my cage. Something was set down on the ground. The footsteps retreated and the door closed once more.

I put a hand through the bars and groped about for the object that had been placed there. My fingers touched a soft, quilted bag with something slender and hard inside.

Lockpicks.

It is quite awkward to kneel inside a cage and open a lock on the outside. Total darkness does not make it any easier. I was glad I'd had a very good teacher.

Once I'd gotten the lock undone, I crawled out of the cage, stood, and stretched. Oh, the relief of a straight spine! Then I made my way to the barn door. It had been left open a crack. I put my ear to it and listened.

I heard a thump, like a stiffened hand meeting a solid mass of flesh and bone. Then a heavier thump, like a body falling to the ground. A voice from the other side of the door spoke my name, so quietly that even a termite dozing in its hole would not have stirred. "Kata?"

"Tomiko?" It was half a guess—it was hard to be sure of an identity from muffled footsteps and a single whispered word. However, it seemed that my guess was right, since the speaker on the other side of the door did not correct me.

"Hurry. It's almost dawn." The door eased open again. Tomiko took my arm and guided me forward. I stepped over a crumpled body that lay on the ground.

The sun had not yet risen, but the darkness was starting to lighten. Instead of swimming in a pool of black ink, we were wading through a swamp of gray forms in a gray mist. Tomiko had planned her route well, as I'd expect of any student of Madame Chiyome. My bare feet felt the trodden earth of a stable yard, then the plowed furrows of a field. Soft grass, ankle height, came next, and after that firm earth again—a path.

By the time we reached a clearing, there was enough light that I could see a figure rise from where it had been concealed under a ridge of stone. My hand moved instinctively toward where my knife should have been, even though I was quite sure I knew who this was and that she was no threat.

"Kata. Thank every god." Arms reached out to take me in a quick, tight embrace. "Oh, I was worried." Masako pulled back to touch my face with gentle fingers. "Are you hurt? Badly?"

I shook my head.

"You have somewhere for us to hide?" Tomiko's voice came out of the dimness at my left.

"This way."

My old schoolmate led us swiftly along an overgrown path. As she walked, she kicked apart an arrow made of three sticks on the ground and later knocked over a few rocks that had been piled into a tower, so I knew she'd been here before and marked her trail.

I wondered if she'd found a cave for us, or was heading deeper into the forest, but she'd planned better than that. Her path took us down a muddy slope. At the end of that slope a quick little river ran. A boat was tied to a sapling that bent and bowed with the strength of the tugging current.

At first both Tomiko and I huddled in the bow, kept from view of prying eyes by a rough cloth cover, while Masako steered the boat downstream. As hours went past and the day lightened, however, she eventually used her paddle to steer the boat to one side, and we felt it bump against a soft bank. "You can sit up now," she said quietly.

Tomiko and I shook off our cover, relieved to draw in breaths of fresh air and move stiff muscles. Masako had taken us under a willow tree, the dangling leaves and drooping branches making a shady shelter. Through their screen, I could glimpse a dense green growth of alders along the bank. Mist was rising off the river with the damp warmth of the morning.

Masako had tied the boat to a root that arched up out of the water. She smiled broadly, reaching this time to hug Tomiko, who blinked in surprise and sat stiffly in her embrace.

"You did wonderfully," Masako said, letting her go. "Here, you must both be starving." From the bottom of the boat she picked up a bundle wrapped in a large, square piece of blue cloth. The cloth was a bit damp, but the baskets inside were dry. Masako pulled the lid off one and handed out balls of sticky rice. I bit into mine hungrily, discovering a salty piece of dried fish in the center. Tomiko took a small bite and chewed thoughtfully.

"Jinnai found me the same day you'd been taken," Masako told me, her fingers busy with the knot of a second bundle. I nodded. I'd hoped he would; I'd certainly paid him well enough to get word to Masako if anything should happen to me. But of course, you could never be certain that an ally, however well paid, would keep up his end of the bargain.

It was something all three of us had been taught at Madame's school. *Trust no friend farther than you can see her. Trust no ally for more than you've paid him.*

"One of the gatekeepers remembered an oxcart leaving in the dead of night, so it wasn't too hard to follow you," Masako went on. She'd pulled the bundle open by now and spread it out on her lap. I smiled.

A deadly little knife in a sheath. A black silk cord that could be tied around a waist. A set of narrow metal bars, some with pointed ends, some with hooks, some hammered into flat shapes like tiny shovels. A simple hair ornament whose stick could twist open to reveal a wicked sliver of a blade. A few small ceramic jars, their mouths sealed shut with wax. Flint and steel and a tinderbox. Finally, several strings of cash, the brass and silver coins threaded together by a cord through the square holes in their centers.

Masako had known exactly what I would need.

"Then I just had to find the boat and get word to Tomiko," she explained as I set about strapping the knife to my forearm, securing the pin in my hair, distributing the other tools among various pockets of my jacket, feeling all the while like a turtle crawling back into its shell. I never felt like myself unarmed.

Tomiko swallowed the mouthful she'd been slowly chewing. "Masako made me a promise," she said, as I slipped some of the metal rods into a narrow pocket along the seam of my sleeve. "In your name."

I nodded. "I'll fulfill it."

Tomiko dropped her eyes to the food in her hand, but did not take another bite. "Right now I'm a runaway. If Madame finds me—"

"Madame will spend the day searching every field and hollow and storehouse around that farm," Masako said briskly. "And that will give us a start."

"A short one." Tomiko applied herself to eating as if she'd suddenly remembered an unfinished job. "I want what was promised to me."

"Now?" I took a second ball of rice. Working for Master Ishikawa, I'd gotten fairly used to regular meals. My empty stomach felt like a well with no bottom.

"I think there's a good chance you won't be alive to give it to me later," Tomiko answered.

Masako frowned. But Tomiko hadn't spoken harshly. She was merely calculating odds. We all did. It was part of our training.

Hidden in a panel of embroidery on the left sleeve of my jacket was the loop and hook that kept a secret pocket shut. I opened the flap and slid out what I kept inside—two rubies and an emerald with a dark, cloudy flaw at its heart.

The jewel Fuku had knocked out of my mouth hadn't been the only one I'd taken from Master Ishikawa. It was a pity, I thought now, that I hadn't added that stone to the ones in this pocket, but I'd been afraid so many objects in there at once would make a noticeable lump.

Not nearly as noticeable, in the end, as a jewel bouncing across the floor mats, but there was no way to fix that now.

I handed all three stones to Tomiko. Even with the emerald's imperfection, it was a valuable hoard. Enough to buy a ninja. I knew, because I'd bought several.

"That could pay for passage across the Inland Sea," I said as Tomiko examined the jewels critically. "Or you can go back to Madame and bargain for your freedom, and she'll let you be."

Tomiko snorted. "Or she could keep the jewels for herself and put me in a cage, like you."

Masako shook her head, and her loose hair swept across the collar of her plain cotton kimono. "I don't think she would. She's honored every bargain Kata's made with her."

"Until now." Tomiko tucked her jewels away into a hidden pocket along the hem of her own jacket.

"Madame didn't come after me because of the girls I've bought from her," I said. "She did it for a client."

Masako and Tomiko turned their faces toward me.

"For Saiko."

Tomiko's fingers paused on the fastening of her pocket. Masako drew in a slow breath. A ripple rocked the boat under us, and the leaves of the willow flickered in a breeze.

Then Tomiko finished what she was doing and patted the pocket smooth. "In that case, I'm leaving now."

"Tomiko." Masako stirred and put out a hand. "You don't have to go, not so quickly. You can come home with me. My husband won't mind. And I can find some work for you to do. Listen—you have choices now. You don't have to be what Madame made you. What she tried to make all of us."

Tomiko looked genuinely astonished. "What else could I be?"

Masako's slow smile spread over her wide, plain face. "Anything. That's the amazing thing, Tomiko. That's what Kata bought for me. For Ozu and the others. Now for you. You can be anything."

Tomiko's forehead only crinkled in further bewilderment. "What else would I *want* to be?"

Masako hesitated, glancing at me. But I had nothing to add. Tomiko's choices were her own now—not for Madame to dictate, not for Masako, not for me.

"You don't understand . . . ," Masako began.

"I understand that Madame will never rest until she's delivered Kata to Saiko. And I don't plan to be caught in the middle." Tomiko slid herself deftly out of the little boat, barely causing it to rock as she stepped to the bank. "Good fortune to you both. You'll need it."

Before she pushed aside the willow leaves, I spoke. "There's no debt between us?"

Tomiko touched her pocket briefly. "None."

She slipped through the leaves and was gone.

"She could have stayed," Masako said in dismay. "I would have taken care of her."

I smiled. Only Masako would think that a girl who knew at least thirty-nine ways to end a life would need her tender care.

"But she's right, you know, Kata. Madame will be searching for you. We need to find a way to keep you safe."

"We need to keep the pearl safe from Saiko."

"Very much the same thing. She found you once, Kata. Where can you hide this time?"

An idea was stirring in my mind. I closed my eyes to see it better, and a picture danced behind my lids—wavy blue lines on a sheet of paper that, somehow, meant the same thing as the heave and slap of heavy, cold water, vast distance, the tang of salt, and the kiss of chilly wind.

"There's nowhere in the world, Kata. There's nowhere she won't go to find you."

"I think the world might be bigger than we knew," I told her.

SIX

I climbed out of the boat and waited beneath the willow tree as Masako retied her bundle and followed me onto the bank. Then she undid the rope, kicking the boat out into the current. A shame to lose it, but tied there, it would only serve as a signpost showing any pursuers where to look for us.

Something caught my eye, a quick flash of white, a flicker of movement through the silver-green screen of long, narrow leaves. I touched Masako's arm, pointed, and pushed the leaves aside.

We were deep in a soggy thicket of alders and more willows, so close there was little room for grass to grow around their roots. Between two bushy trees, its eyes yellow in the sun, a white fox sat watching us.

Masako twitched in surprise, but I deliberately relaxed the hand that had moved toward my new knife. I hadn't been expecting the fox, but I was not surprised to meet her.

She had a way of turning up when I was unsure of my path.

I had seen her last two years ago, when I had become the pearl's guardian. Now she turned and trotted off, her tail a flag that we could follow.

Masako glanced at me in question, and I nodded. We set out after our guide.

Somehow the fox always found firm ground to stand on and places where we could push between leafy branches. Even so, we were scratched and disheveled and weary of slapping biting insects by the time the creature led us out onto a road.

It would be better called a track, hardly wide enough for one oxcart, the ruts faint and overgrown with grass. Even so, I winced to feel so exposed. People had made this; therefore people might see us here. I'd felt safer in the trees.

But I had learned to trust the white fox, whose tail was now vanishing around a curve ahead. Well, trust was too strong a word, perhaps. The fox had never led me into harm—and yet I knew I was not her concern. It was the pearl she watched over, the pearl she wanted to protect. That meant protecting me as well, for now.

And so I followed her. For now.

She led us along the path, which narrowed as we went, scrubby bushes and tall grasses closing in, weeds growing thicker underfoot. I kept my ears alert, and the twitter and rustle of birds in the branches (somehow they were not afraid of the fox) told me the forest was at peace around us.

Our track took us uphill, growing rockier and more rugged, carved more deeply into the earth. Mist gathered, cool and damp in my lungs and on my lips.

Ahead, a smooth gray shape loomed out of the greenery. I stopped; behind me, I heard the oily hiss of Masako's blade sliding from its sheath. I raised a hand, palm down, to let her know that what I'd seen was no threat—and neither was its twin on the other side of the path.

The fox sat between two statues of dogs, their stone pelts overgrown with lichen, the teeth in their open mouths snarling through moss. Beyond them I could see the upright posts that had once supported the lintel of a ceremonial gate—and there it was, or what was left of it, fallen across the path, rotting into the forest floor.

"A shrine?" I asked the fox. "I don't think prayers will help us at the moment." Not with Madame hunting us.

The fox tilted her head, gave me an impatient look through narrowed eyes, and darted into the undergrowth, leaving us no chance to follow.

"She wants us to . . . visit the shrine?" Masako asked doubtfully from behind me.

I studied the fallen gate and the neglected statues, and let my eye travel farther along the path to a set of stone stairs laid into the hillside, cracked and worn, damp with the mist that obscured whatever lay at the top.

"I think she's telling us it's a safe place to stay," I answered Masako. "For a few days, at least." And it was also a place where I might be able to find the kind of help I would need next.

No priests served at this shrine anymore; no villagers came to make prayers or give offerings. We climbed the slippery stairs to reach a compound thick with cedar and pine. A basin at the top of the stairs was choked with needles; a thin puddle of rainwater lay on top. Beyond it stood the shrine's main building, or what was left of it. Two walls were still standing, and half a roof slanted down over them. Whatever spirit once dwelled here had obviously fled.

Even so, Masako paused at the basin to clean her hands and lift a mouthful of water to her lips, showing respect. She glanced at me, but I shrugged. I wasn't here to beg a favor or plead for mercy from the gods; I was here to fulfill a mission they had laid upon me. They would have to take me as I was.

I turned slowly, eyeing the tumbled shrine, the enveloping trees, the ground thick with layer upon layer of golden needles that looked as if they had been undisturbed for years.

I could not see any watchers. I could not hear them. But I was sure they were nearby. This was just the kind of place they liked. I raised my voice a little and reminded myself to ask, not to order.

"I request the honor of your presence," I called into the crisscrossed maze of green needles and gray mist overhead. "I want to make a bargain with you."

The trees quivered. Not the faintest trace of wind blew against my face, but in every direction, pine and cedar needles quaked.

Behind my right shoulder (where she had placed herself, out of old habit, so that her own right arm would be free to swing a weapon), Masako drew in a breath.

Black wings flickered among the dull, deep green and

the swirls of mist. A faint murmuring arose, curious and urgent. Then a birdlike shape lifted from a branch and winged through the air toward us.

Dark as a crow, agile as a hummingbird, the tengu swooped to a spot just level with my eyes and hovered there. It had a bird's body, but two human eyes regarded me over the dull yellow beak. On the end of each black wing there was a five-fingered hand.

The right hand held a curved sword, more elegant than anything made by a human smith. It looked sharp enough to slice wind.

I put my hands together and bowed. Masako did the same. The tengu swished its sword impatiently through the air. It wanted to know why I had called.

"Will you do me the honor of carrying a message?" I asked, careful to keep my tone respectful. Tengu were notoriously touchy; I'd known it from legend and found it out for myself on more than one occasion over the last two years. "And I'll need two friends of yours as well."

The tengu narrowed its eyes.

"The usual payment, of course." I added another little bow, for good measure.

The tengu sneered at me. I never knew how they managed that with the beak, but they did. Then it nodded.

I told my messenger who to seek and then kicked aside the needles at my feet until I came to bare earth. With the point of a stick, I sketched a few characters and a rough map in the dirt. The tengu eyed them briefly and nodded again. Their memories were remarkable; I knew it would reproduce the message perfectly when it reached its destination. And that meant no scrap of rice paper or bit of rolled silk to carry, which was a risk avoided.

The tengu extended the hand that was not holding the sword.

I folded my arms. "Payment after the job. Not before."

A pinecone was lobbed at my head from above, but I was prepared for it, and batted it aside.

The tengu scowled. I lifted one eyebrow.

Suddenly it dipped a wing to pivot in midair and dart back to the branch it had come from. There was a rustle among the leaves and a squabble of conversation, mutters and caws that my ear could almost, but not quite, make into words.

Masako let out a slightly shaky breath. "I never get used to that," she murmured. "Are they always watching you?"

"Always. As long as I have it." Ignoring the urge to reach inside the jacket and touch the pocket with the pearl, I left my hands at my sides as I used one toe to scuff out the message I had written and scatter evergreen needles back over the ground.

Masako had taken in its meaning before I erased the characters. "So we'll meet them here in three days' time?"

I nodded.

"And what will we do when they get here?"

A plan was evolving in my mind, but I wasn't ready to speak of it, not yet. "First we'll need supplies," I told her. And one of the things we'd have to buy would be three flasks of rice wine. It would not do to start a journey in debt to a tengu. They tended to be quite intolerant about that kind of thing.

⸸ ⸸ ⸸

Three days later, an old woman, stumping along with a stick, came between the statues of the dogs, climbed over the fallen gate, and began to mount the stairs. She did it fairly briskly, despite the years that showed in her hunched shoulders and the gray strands of hair that straggled out from beneath her round straw hat.

Once at the top, the crone laid her stick aside and dipped her hands briefly in the basin. I eyed those hands—unwrinkled and strong—and whistled softly between my teeth.

The newcomer pulled off her round straw hat and looked up to the branch above her head where I was lying, facedown, so that I could see everything that went on below me.

"You should wear longer sleeves," I told her.

She spread her hands out to look at them critically, nodded, and settled herself among the knobby roots of my tree, adjusting the skirts of her worn and patched kimono.

"They're coming," Masako called softly from her perch above me in a crook of the tree. "Along the river. At least I think so. The mist makes it hard to see."

Mist clung to this shrine as though it were a steamy bathhouse, as we'd found in the last few days. It kept things damp and made it hard to coax a fire into life, but it was also useful for concealment. Perhaps the mists were what had hidden us from Madame and her girls, who must be searching for us. Or perhaps it was some old power in this place, which was why the fox had led us here. I didn't know, which made me anxious and restless to be gone. I didn't like relying on luck, or vanished gods, or mists. But we could not leave before our companions joined us.

A few moments later, I saw that Masako was right. I could catch bright glimpses of yellow and scarlet through the trees, like a fan flashing open and shut with a flick of the wrist. Before long two new arrivals were mounting the steps, slender figures in gaudy kimonos, hand in hand. One held a traveler's staff over her shoulder.

"Yuki?" the one holding the staff called when they reached the shrine compound. "You got one, too?"

The traveler resting beneath my tree reached into her belt and pulled out a black feather. Aki, who'd spoken, had one behind her ear, nearly invisible against her sleek dark hair.

"Are we early?" Okiko asked as she dipped her hands into the basin, raised the water to her mouth, and nudged her twin to do the same.

Yuki shook her head, and I jumped down. Okiko flicked her knife out before I landed, and Aki had her staff braced in both hands.

"Kata." Okiko shook her head and tucked the knife back in her sleeve. Aki lowered one tip of the staff—weighted with lead, I noticed—back to the ground. "It's not enough to call us away from a very profitable market town?"

"You have to stop our hearts as well?" Aki added.

Masako climbed down more sedately. Yuki smiled a quick, quiet smile.

Back on solid ground, Masako beamed at Yuki and pulled each twin into an embrace. "You're doing well, then?" she asked warmly. "When are you coming back to the coast? Ozu would love to see you perform."

I took a careful look along what could be seen of the trail to the shrine, making sure no one had followed the two newcomers.

"Quite well. Watch this!" Okiko pulled her obi loose from around her waist and shrugged off her kimono. Under it she wore loose trousers and a short jacket similar to mine. "Our newest trick."

She dropped to one knee and Aki stepped lightly up onto her cupped hands. When Okiko surged to her feet, her sister was thrown into the air, where she tucked her body into a somersault and then flung her arms wide, the skirts and sleeves of her kimono rippling out in a red and gold sunburst. She very nearly looked as if she'd take flight, but instead she landed neatly on her feet, and the two bowed as Masako grinned and Yuki softly applauded.

"The crowds love it!" Aki said.

"It's worth more coins than the rest of the act put together," Okiko said.

"And people are still coming to buy your herbs?" Masako asked Yuki after giving her a hug of her own.

Yuki nodded.

"And your husband?" Aki asked Masako. "Does he still make—"

"—those steamed cakes? From sweet bean paste and rice flour, with the hydrangea juice?" Okiko finished the question.

"The best in the province!" Masako's smile spread even wider.

I had lived with these girls, knelt beside them at meals, faced them in the practice yard as we'd wielded bamboo swords and then blunt blades and finally weapons with true edges. I could remember Yuki, perhaps eight years old, grinding dried roots to powder in a mortar no larger than her hand. Aki and Okiko sleeping on the same mat, breathing the same air, probably dreaming the same dreams. Masako combing the younger girls' hair, tying their obis, bandaging their wounds, wiping their tears.

I had despised them. Masako's kindness had seemed only a weakness. Yuki's silent fascination with poisons and potions could never make up for her slowness with a blade. Aki and Okiko needed each other, and I'd believed the instructors who told us a deadly flower should never need anybody.

They had not been my friends. I'd had no friends. I'd had opponents whom I'd left in the dust of the practice yard. I'd had rivals—until the day, at last, when I had none.

But on the first night when I'd begun to understand what it would mean to be the guardian of the pearl, these girls had fought for me. Without them, I'd have been food for a demon before I'd even discovered what the treasure in my pocket truly was, or what it could do.

"And what does that husband of yours say when you go off for a few days?" Okiko teased Masako. "Do you tell him you're going to visit riverbank people?"

"Riffraff like us?" Aki chimed in. "Acrobats and a wandering herbalist and—"

"—a deadly flower?" Both twins laughed.

"I told him I had to see an old friend," Masako answered. She was not laughing with them now. "One whose debt I'm in."

All four girls turned their eyes toward me. Aki drew the black feather from behind her ear. Yuki stroked hers through her fingers.

When the gods had granted me my freedom, or when I had snatched it away from Madame Chiyome and the warlord she'd sold me to—I was still not quite sure which of those things had happened—I had not been able to forget the faces of the girls who'd fought for me. And so I'd bought them.

Ninjas were not cheap, but neither was I. Master Ishikawa had paid me well (better, in fact, than he had known) for the work I'd done. I would have been rich by now, if I'd saved it all. And so I was, even though I'd spent everything I'd taken.

Rich in favors owed.

"What do you need, Kata?" Aki asked.

Again, I restrained my hands from touching the jewel inside my pocket—the one I'd never traded or sold.

"I want you to help me save the pearl," I said. "I'm going to take it over the sea."

It took Masako and me a little time to convince the other girls that I could, indeed, reach the lands that lay beyond the horizon. And then the two of us unpacked the supplies we'd gathered in the small marketplaces of the nearby towns.

We'd ventured out cautiously, Masako doing the purchasing while I stayed out of sight, keeping watch in case one of the shopkeepers or travelers or farmers selling rice or mushrooms or melons was actually a shadow warrior in disguise. But everyone seemed to be just what they appeared to be. And if the back of my neck prickled constantly, or my hands twitched again and again toward the knife in my sleeve, well, perhaps I was only on edge, knowing who was looking for me and why.

Now our purchases were spread out on the ground: three pairs of loose trousers and three short jackets, all made of cotton dyed with indigo, all well-worn already. One straw hat, such as a peasant might wear in the fields, and two hoods. Yuki combed the rice flour out of her hair, the twins stowed their bright clothing in a corner of the shrine, and before long I was looking at three copies of myself.

Masako was half a hand too tall, Yuki's skin was a shade too fair, and Okiko had her sister for a companion, now dressed in Masako's plain cotton kimono. Still, someone searching the roads and tracks and riverways of this province for a girl in men's clothing with a pearl in her pocket might well mistake any of the other three for me.

Especially because each had a pearl in her pocket.

They were actually glossy white beads, wound with golden wire, that I'd pried loose from a hair ornament Masako had purchased. They might pass for pearls on a quick inspection—and if it came to more than a quick inspection, we were in greater trouble than a jewel could solve.

Yuki, we decided, would set off toward a monastery in the mountains. There, a monk named Tosabo had been teaching a novice for the past few years. That novice was Saiko's brother, and it would be easy for her to believe that I'd seek his help to keep the pearl safe.

Aki and Okiko would head away from the coast, deeper into the wilderness, where it would become impossible to track them. And Masako would make her way back toward the harbor town where we'd both been living.

"And you, Kata?" Okiko asked. "Where will you go?"

Two friends can keep a secret, if one of them is dead.

I trusted these girls as far as I trusted anyone. But they had no need to know where I'd be heading.

"My own way," I answered.

Masako laughed. "Don't you always?"

At the shrine, I watched them all leave. Then I laid three flasks of rice wine on the steps. A vigorous fluttering in the pine needles overhead told me that the payment had been noticed and would be collected.

The other four girls would spend at least some of their time on the open roads, buying provisions from farms and asking their way at roadside inns. They'd need to be careful but not too careful, offering a trail that a watcher might pick up, but not enough of a trail that they'd be caught.

I, on the other hand, spent the rest of that day as far from any road as I could get, following thread-thin and winding hunters' paths, forcing my way through shrubs, wading calf-deep through swamps, and earning a night's rest that I did not get. Instead of sleeping as darkness fell, I lay curled up by the ashes of my fire, chilled by the light drizzle that was starting to drift down from the clouds, listening to something in the bushes that should not have been there.

Leaves rubbed on leaves. A twig scraped against a branch. All innocent sounds, the sort that might have been made by a small bird hopping from twig to twig—except that no bird had alighted on that bush in the time it had taken for my fire to burn down.

Had she found me, then?

Had it all been for nothing, summoning my friends and sending them out across the province? Had Madame laughed at our feeble efforts to evade her search and focused on me like a cat selecting the plumpest mouse?

Time to find out.

In one movement, I surged up to a crouch, kicking the fire as I went, startling the sleepy coals into a blaze. My back was to the flames, so they could not dazzle my eyes, but hopefully the watcher in the undergrowth could see nothing but glare for the moment.

A moment would be long enough.

SEVEN

I launched myself at the rustling bush, colliding with a soft yet solid mass. There was a dark, prickly struggle. Twigs snapped. Branches bent, then slapped back at anything in their way. I jabbed my elbow into something and heard a painful whoosh of breath. Fastening my hand in a mass of short hair, I wrestled my watcher out of the greenery and threw her full length on the ground by the fire.

"How many more?" I dropped to my knees to seize the hair again, yanking my opponent's head back, drawing my blade and setting it to her throat—

—except that it was *his* throat. Wide eyes blinked up at me from a familiar face, blackened with dirt for better concealment. A voice I knew croaked out, "Kata—stop! Please! It's me!"

I was startled, but not enough to drop the knife or let him go. Jinnai? Jinnai, spying on me from the bushes?

Spying on me for Ishikawa? For Madame?

Under the surprise came a jolt of disappointment. We'd worked together, and worked well. Master Sakuma had not been the only merchant the two of us had robbed. Over time, I'd come to trust that he would at least keep his end of a bargain.

Our bargain had merely called for him to get word to Masako if anything should happen to me. It had not included stalking me through the wilderness.

"How many more?" I repeated, pinning his head more firmly to the ground.

"Just me," he whispered hoarsely. "Truth. On my honor."

"On your honor as a thief?"

The corner of his mouth quirked up. "As the best thief Master Ishikawa owns. Come, Kata. Let me go."

"Why should I?" I demanded, my back prickling with vulnerability. Was anyone going to come to his aid? Or would his companions let me cut his throat as penance for being fool enough to be caught?

Now one of Jinnai's eyebrows quirked along with his lips. "Because if you kill me, I can't tell you why I'm here."

Curiosity is a good servant, but a bad master.

I knew better than to let a desire for information rule me. Was Jinnai more of a risk alive or dead? That was all that should be in my mind.

"You can always kill me later," Jinnai pointed out. "But if I'm dead, I can't answer any questions. Not one."

I let my breath out slowly between my teeth. If Jinnai

had confederates hidden in the woods, they did not seem inclined to leap to his defense. So perhaps it would be safe to hear whatever he had to say.

I moved my knife an inch away from his skin.

"Can I sit up?" he asked.

I moved the knife farther away, though I kept the tip pointed in his direction. He eyed it warily as he maneuvered himself slowly into a sitting position and winced.

"I knew you were fast, Kata, but I didn't know you could move like a hungry snake. Next time I'll stay farther back."

Next time? Did he imagine he'd get any opportunity to do this again? "Why are you here?" I asked impatiently. Maybe if I cut off one of his ears he'd get to the point faster.

In our scuffle, a branch had caught him across the face, leaving a swollen weal that was beginning to trickle blood. He patted it gingerly with his fingertips. "I was worried about you."

I could feel my face stiffen in astonishment.

"I wanted to help you at Master Ishikawa's, but there was nothing I could do. So I got word to your friend. As you asked."

"That was *all* I asked," I reminded him.

"And then I followed her."

Masako must have been out of practice, letting this oaf of a thief creep along a road behind her.

"The river gave me a little trouble, it's true, but luckily I caught sight of you and your friend in a market town nearby. And earlier today, I was under an old bridge when

I spotted three Katas heading off in different directions. None of them looked quite right, though. So I waited until you came along. I've been behind you ever since."

I scowled at him. "You did all that because you were *worried* about me?" Skepticism dripped off each word.

"Well." He looked a little sheepish, as if I'd caught him in a lie he'd never expected to work. "And I wondered why you were worth so much. I saw the jewels on Master Ishikawa's table."

Now that sounded more plausible.

"Did you steal something?" He leaned forward. "Something you weren't supposed to, I mean. And Master Ishikawa found out? That's why he sold you to—whoever took you?"

"No," I said coldly, which was true, at least in part. I *had* stolen from our master—and he must know it, since Fuku had knocked that jewel out of my mouth like a loose tooth—but that was not why he'd sold me.

The eager interest in Jinnai's face made me think he might be speaking the truth. If he had honestly wanted to know why I was so valuable, he might well be here in the woods alone. He wouldn't have wanted to share his find.

I sat back a little farther, creating more space between my blade and his heart.

To my considerable surprise, he smiled at me, a wide grin that lit his narrow, dirty, clever face. "And, of course, I'm in love with you," he said cheerfully.

A few hours later, in the gray light of dawn, I had a decision to make.

"Kata?" Jinnai asked plaintively from the other side of the clearing. "You're not going to leave me here, are you?"

Early on, Master Ishikawa had assigned Jinnai to work with me. I had not, at first, been pleased. *A risk shared is a risk doubled.* I'd been taught that working alone was safest.

But I'd quickly come to see how well Jinnai's skills meshed with my own.

I could leave him on his back after the quickest of sparring matches, but he could pick a lock faster than me. I'd mastered every weapon; he'd memorized every winding lane and wandering alley of the Takedas' city. I knew how to make myself all but invisible; he knew how to make himself popular.

No one knew me. Everybody knew Jinnai.

A smile here, a nod there. A favor done, a gift given. The beggars greeted him. The fishermen waved to him. Their wives giggled at him from behind their hands. Even those as despicable as butchers and tanners dared to speak to him; outcasts hauling filth from latrines to the river didn't scuttle aside too far as he passed them. The very guard dogs wagged their tails at him.

And no one thought of him when screens were slit, when locks were picked, when coins were missing. Because everyone *liked* him.

I'd never thought of charm as a weapon before I met Jinnai.

Last night, after his ridiculous declaration, I'd tied

his hands (in front of him, so he would not be in pain), attached the end of the cord to a sapling to keep him in one place, and returned to my fire, alone.

Around me, the forest had settled back into peace. The soft rasping, trilling, fluting calls of insects and birds drifted through the trees, the flutter of wings and the patter of small feet echoing so that they seemed as if they were made by beasts much larger than mice or voles or frogs or nightingales.

From Jinnai's anxious breathing, I'd guessed that he might be thinking the same thing. How many nights had this city-born boy spent in a forest? To him, the tiny creatures of the darkness probably sounded like stealthy wolves or ravenous bears.

Among all the sounds that wove together to make up the nighttime hush, I had heard no hint of anything human. Jinnai had likely been telling the truth, at least when he'd said he was alone.

I'd also heard no hint of anything inhuman. No ghostly whispers, no demon laughter. Nothing to suggest that the pearl in my pocket had stirred the local bakemono to life, unless a few of the rustling wings belonged to curious tengu. But if so, they were keeping their distance. I could only hope that the calm would last.

As for Jinnai's other words—of course I knew them to be false. He was simply trying to use his charm on me, as I'd seen him use it so often before. He must have hoped that a claim of something as absurd as love would confuse me. Distract me. Keep me from remembering why he was truly here.

He believed I had something of value. He'd followed me to steal it. He was a thief. It was all he knew how to do.

"Didn't you guess? You must have guessed," he said now, leaning against his tree trunk and eyeing me curiously.

I snorted and busied myself kicking apart the ashes of my fire. With a sharpened stick, I dug into the dirt beneath it to retrieve a bundle of cloth. I'd soaked it in water last night and wrapped it around a handful of rice. Now the rice, though cool, was soft enough to eat.

"You notice everything. I've never seen you miss a detail. Close your eyes and tell me what I'm wearing."

I didn't close my eyes, but I didn't look up from my meal. "Indigo jacket. Gray trousers. Socks that aren't white anymore. Sandals. The right one's been mended twice. Brass earring in your ear—your left ear. Ivory amulet under the jacket that you should keep better hidden."

"See? And you tell me you never noticed the way I looked at you?"

If I'd never noticed such a thing, it meant there was nothing *to* notice. I swallowed the last of the rice, leaving none for my captive—if he wanted food, he should have carried it himself. Next I picked up my round straw hat, tied the strings to secure it under my chin, and let it hang down my back.

Then I got to my feet.

"Kata?" Jinnai sat up straight. The bruise I'd left on his face four days ago had faded to brown and yellow, and the red weal made by the branch in our struggle last night cut across it, straight as if drawn with a brush. His clothes were muddy from our tussle and from whatever sleep he'd gotten among the roots of his tree. "You wouldn't," he said, clearly unconvinced by his own words. "You wouldn't actually . . ."

Leave him there? Of course I shouldn't leave him there. What I ought to do was kill him.

I had a mission. He was a threat to it. *Every threat to your mission must be eliminated.*

Jinnai's confusion was slowly giving way to alarm.

The kind thing, in fact, would be to cut his throat quickly. It would be less cruel than leaving him where he was, at the mercy of hunger and thirst and predators. Oh, maybe he'd attract the attention of some charcoal burner or hunter or old wife gathering roots and herbs, and maybe whoever found him would set him free instead of killing him for his earring and his amulet and whatever coins might be in his pockets. But maybe not. In any case, he'd face a long, cold, hungry wait for a rescue that might never come.

To hesitate was weak, but I did not like the thought. I'd dodged Takeda guards with Jinnai. I'd stood on his shoulders to scale walls. I'd relied on him to distract dogs while I worked my way through hedges. Must I leave him to what would likely be a lingering death simply because he'd plotted to steal from me?

I'd been living among thieves for two years, and I knew that any one of them would have done the same. Jinnai had been faithful to his training; that was all.

He'd be faithful to that training no matter what, I thought. And that meant I didn't need to kill him—or leave him. There was another way.

I slid my knife from its sheath along my forearm.

"Kata? I really think you ought to listen to me now," Jinnai said, wide-eyed, twisting his hands in his bonds as apprehension quivered in every word. "I can see I was in the wrong to follow you. I won't make that mistake again. But you don't give a man many chances to declare his devotion. You must realize that. And of course I knew you'd never believe me. But I think you'll regret—"

In three steps I was beside his tree. I dropped to one knee, brought the knife swiftly down, and slashed the cords with which I'd tied his hands.

With a groan, Jinnai flopped onto his back among a litter of twigs and dead leaves. "Don't do that to a man," he said feebly. "I won't have any heart left to love you with if you make it burst with terror."

I rose to my feet. "Just—," I started to say, but stopped.

He quirked an eyebrow at me from where he lay. "Just what?"

Just remember I could have killed you, I thought.

"Just don't slow me down," I said as I turned and strode off between two trees.

He followed me, as I'd known he would. He wouldn't leave me, not as long as he still thought I had something he could steal.

EIGHT

I didn't know this landscape as well as I did that of the province where I had grown up, in Madame's school, studying Madame's maps. And Jinnai was no help at all. As I'd suspected, this was the first time he'd been outside the walls of the harbor city where he had been born.

"If you wanted to know how to find a particular teahouse in the pleasure district, I could tell you easily," he explained, keeping close behind as I ventured along a narrow, rocky path that might have been made by hunters or by deer. "Or the alleys down by the wharfs? I can find my way there blindfolded and with my ears stopped up, just by the smell. But out here—are there snakes? Is there a reason you don't want to take the main road?"

"Yes." I let go of a branch. He ducked as it whipped back over his head.

"You wouldn't want to tell me what it is, would you?"

"No."

"Or what there is about you that's so valuable someone paid Master Ishikawa more than what a shipload of excellent rice wine is worth?"

"No."

"Well, I didn't think so. You should be more careful of him, you know, Kata. He's not a person you want angry at you. About the snakes?"

I knew the direction I wanted to go, and I kept at it, guided by the angle of the sun, picking my way from one broken-backed trail to another, forcing my body through scrubby undergrowth and along muddy streams, hiding only the time I heard feet somewhere in the distance. A hunter after game? Or a ninja after me?

Jinnai could keep his tongue still enough when it mattered. The footsteps faded without either of us catching a glimpse of their maker.

The other girls would be traveling more swiftly and easily, and also a bit more conspicuously. Masako should reach the city a full day, perhaps two, before I would. Then she'd disappear neatly into her old life, and anyone following her trail would find that it had gone cold. That should leave me free to enter and find my way down to the harbor, to choose a ship that would take me and the pearl out of Madame's reach, out of Saiko's.

I hoped.

And what would I do with Jinnai, then? Push him into the ocean, perhaps. It would be satisfying.

We spent our second night on a cliff overlooking the harbor, a bowl of sea scooped out between the encircling arms of two mountains. I'd lived the past two years in the town by that harbor, but this was the first time I'd surveyed it from such a height—a jumble of roofs, thatch and tile, looking like things thrown pell-mell into a bag. As the morning light strengthened, I perched on an outcrop of crumbling rock, my knees under my chin, studying the scene below me.

I could see the broad avenue that began at Ryujin's shrine and ran downhill to the jetty, where trading ships and the largest fishing boats were moored. My eyes traced the river winding through a gap in the mountains to cut the city in two. There were also three main roads leading through the heights and into the warren of streets and alleys.

Each road passed through a gap in the rugged hills, and in each gap was a wooden fort where soldiers kept an eye on all of the traffic. Where the river entered the city, it flowed through a stone gate watched by more armed men.

I didn't need to see those men up close to know that each had the chrysanthemum of the Takeda family embroidered on his jacket or lacquered on his armor. Ishikawa Goemon might rule the city's underworld, but the Takeda family ruled everything else. Nothing went into the city by land or water without their knowledge—and without paying handsomely for the privilege.

At least, that's what the Takedas thought.

"Not the roads," Jinnai said, as if reading my mind. "What about the river? I know a few flatboat men who owe me a favor, or would like to have me owe them one.

But are you sure that's where you want to go?"

He sat at the foot of a dead, gray, wind-gnarled cedar, his gaze moving back and forth between the city and me.

"Two minutes after we're back, Master Ishikawa will know about it," he continued, his face more serious than usual. "I think even the rats report to him. He won't be any too pleased with me, since I didn't have his permission to leave. But you . . . *Did* you steal from him? Actually, it doesn't much matter if you did or not. You're valuable, Kata. He knows it. What's to keep him from trying to sell you again? He's a dangerous man. Haven't you ever looked at his hands?"

It was such an unexpected question that it captured my full attention, which was probably what Jinnai had intended.

"My mother always told me that hands are important. For people like us." He stretched his own out before him in the sunlight and flexed the fingers, studying them critically. "She always bandaged up every little cut and took out every splinter. A thief's hands are his life. That's what she said. And she taught me that hands show the soul."

I dropped my gaze to my own hands. Strong. Calluses from a sword hilt along the base of the thumb and the pads of the fingers. White scars over more than one knuckle.

Then I thought of Sakuma's soft, plump hand reaching for the place where he hid his treasures.

And Master Ishikawa's hands? I'd last seen them sorting jewels in lamplight. They had long, pale fingers, narrow at the tips. Perfectly clean nails. Careful and precise.

What was that supposed to tell me about his soul?

"I saw him catch a bird once," Jinnai told me. "A sparrow that had blundered into his room somehow. It was flying into screens and walls, trying to escape. He just reached out and—took it. Quicker than anything I've ever seen. He held it in those hands. A tiny brown thing. So frightened. And he—"

Jinnai's own hands knotted into fists.

"Be careful of him, Kata."

An actual shudder inched up my spine and clawed its way over my scalp. Impatiently, I turned away to study the traffic along the nearest road.

My current mission had nothing to do with Master Ishikawa. That did not mean I'd forgotten his betrayal, but Jinnai's warnings and his gruesome little story were nothing but a distraction from what I needed to do next.

On the road below us, women lugged baskets and men carried bundles strung between two poles. Oxcarts trundled up to the fort and back down the slope into the city. One cart in particular, its contents concealed under a heavy cover, caught my eye.

I rose and began to pick my way back down the slope we had climbed the day before, aiming to intersect the road along which that cart was making its slow way. Jinnai followed. "Well, if we must," he said ruefully at my back. "At least a road will be easier on my sandals. But we're not going to simply stroll up to that fort, are we? Kata? Are we?"

We broke free of the trees not many yards ahead of the cart. Its driver, a mountainous hulk of a man with a badly scarred face, had stopped to let his beast stick its snuffling nose into a trickle of a stream that ran across the road.

I came to a halt, casting my gaze up and down the roadway, empty except for the cart, the ox, and the driver.

"We," I said shortly to Jinnai, "are not going anywhere."

While he frowned in puzzlement, a man took a few steps out from behind the thick trunk of an oak.

"Well timed," Commander Otani said. "And well met." A black feather had been tucked into the belt that held his plain brown jacket closed at the waist. He'd had the sense to conceal his battered armor under unremarkable clothes, but anyone with eyes to see would notice how straight he stood, how he kept his hands free, how deftly he balanced as he picked his way over roots and rocks and leaped down to the road's surface.

He no longer wore his hair in a samurai's neat topknot, although he'd retained the vanity of a mustache, long and flowing, carefully combed. Warriors did cherish their mustaches. If one lost his head on the battlefield and an enemy carried it away in triumph, at least the sweeping black facial hair would tell the world that the dead man was a samurai, not a commoner—or worse, a woman.

But it wasn't only the mustache or the two swords at his side that announced what this man was. He moved like a warrior but was dressed like a farmer, and that would show anyone who was paying attention that he was a masterless fighter. A ronin.

"Of course you did not keep us waiting, Flower," he said cheerfully. He knew my name perfectly well, but the second or third time I'd hired him to help with one of Master Ishikawa's jobs, he'd come up with the nickname. It seemed to amuse him, or maybe all that amused him was that it annoyed me. "Your message didn't say there'd be two of you," he went on. "A change in plans?"

"No change." I returned my gaze to Jinnai, whose body had snapped to attention with Otani's appearance. A sharp sliver of a knife was in his hand, and I hadn't even seen him draw it.

I reached out casually while his eyes were still on the ronin and pinched the nerve at the wrist, just where the thumb joins the hand. Jinnai gasped in shock as his fingers, suddenly strengthless, let the knife fall. I kicked it into the stream, seized two handfuls of the thief's jacket, and thrust him at Otani. He grabbed the boy by the shoulders, both to restrain him and prevent the two of them from falling flat in the muddy road.

"Keep him," I told Otani, who, a full handspan taller than Jinnai, looked at me over the thief's head. "Don't hurt him," I added, a bit reluctantly. Why should I care if Otani damaged the thief? Still, if I'd wanted him injured, I could have done that in the forest. "But don't let him follow me, either."

"Kata!" Jinnai protested indignantly. "What are you—"

Otani clamped a large, rough hand over the boy's mouth. "Certainly. Delighted to do you the service. May I assume our usual fee?"

I slipped a hand into my belt and slid out a string of silver coins. Since Otani's hands were occupied, I stepped forward and tucked his payment into the folds of his own belt.

Then I met Jinnai's outraged gaze, but I had no words for him. I simply could not let him imperil my mission.

"Excellent," Otani said, shifting his grip on Jinnai's arm and twisting it up behind his back to stop his struggles. "Such a pity we have no time to chat, Flower, but I prefer not to be seen this close to the city. I hear that Lord Takeda is less than pleased with my activities in his province lately. Noritomo will take you the rest of the—ah!" Jinnai had stamped on his foot. "Do stop wriggling. Yes, I said I wouldn't hurt you, but I'm not all that trustworthy. Good fortune!" he called as I headed toward the oxcart a bit farther along the road. I lifted a hand in response and farewell.

The hulking driver did not even turn his head as Otani dragged Jinnai into the undergrowth and I crawled beneath the rough cloth that covered the straw in his cart. A hollow had been dug into the dried grass. I nestled into it. The cart jolted into motion, bumping into the rutted tracks of the road. We plodded and creaked uphill for a time before the driver stopped to pay his toll at the hill fort. I felt the cart's motion change as we headed downhill toward the town I'd left in a different oxcart only a few days before.

　　　　　　❀　❀　❀

When the ox stopped moving and the driver got off, the cart rocking and groaning under his bulk, I stirred. And when Otani's man slapped the side of the cart in passing, I was ready to slide quickly out.

Noritomo had pulled the cart into a narrow alley alongside an inn. He was now strolling toward the establishment's front door, as if he had nothing more than a cool cup of rice wine on his mind and was utterly unaware of the bedraggled figure crawling out of his straw.

Shaking dust and wisps of grass from my clothes, tucking my hair under my hat, I headed in the opposite direction.

While in the cart, I'd had time to take care of a few things. My clothes were now even more ripped and ragged than my journey through the forest and the battle with the two-tailed cat had left them. One of the ceramic jars Masako had brought me had contained soot, and a bit smeared well over my face and hands had darkened my skin. Another pot held pine pitch. A pinch of that, secured to my upper lip, twisted my mouth in a permanent grimace that was quite repulsive. I saw the gazes of passersby skate over my face and away, and I felt quite satisfied.

If you can't be invisible, become someone no one wants to look at.

A pebble slipped between my foot and the sole of my sandal gave me a convincing hobble, and, all in all, I looked very little like the ninja Madame and her girls would be seeking, or the thief who had served Master Ishikawa for so many months. Careful not to pause and stare, I limped along, casting quick glances from under my hat to discover where the oxcart had taken me.

It was one of the poorer quarters of the city, that was easy to see, with row upon row of houses huddled shoulder to shoulder, their thatched roofs nearly touching. I saw no familiar landmarks, but there was one thing that was easy about this town—going downhill would unfailingly lead you to the sea.

So I made my awkward way past mostly naked brats playing in muddy ditches and their older sisters chasing them, beggars limping even slower than I was, shops selling watered wine and withered plums, a blind man plucking the strings of a biwa and chanting a story to an audience of two. Perhaps he couldn't tell what kind of a neighborhood he'd wandered into, and was vainly hoping for a coin to fall at his feet.

With my halting gait, I was slower than usual, and the afternoon light was beginning to mellow and turn shades of gold and peach before I reached the harbor.

It was tempting to straighten up and walk briskly, but I did not hurry. Past the merchants' warehouses filled with rice and wine, silk and indigo, millet and oranges and melons, there was a strand of stony beach, littered with driftwood and fish guts and twists of rope made of wisteria vine. Wharves bristled into the murky water, and a wide wooden jetty stretched out into the deep. Alongside both were what I'd come looking for—the ships.

Small fishing boats clustered around the wharves to unload their catch, piling fish and eel and abalone and urchins onto the bare wooden planks. They were like tiny darting sandpipers beside the hulk of the warships, anchored farther out, most with a wooden tower for archers and the Takeda chrysanthemum marked on their sails.

Neither warships nor fishing boats would serve my purpose, however, and nor did the brightly lacquered pleasure craft for the warlord's family nor the bulky vessels that toted bags and bundles of tax rice up and down the coast. Nor did the bathship permanently anchored at one wharf, smoke puffing from the cabin on deck where water was heated.

But moored at the far end of the jetty was a larger ship. No pleasure craft, this; its planks were weather-beaten, its two sails worn. Nor was it a small thing built to hug the bays and inlets of the coast. This one looked like the kind of vessel that would bring back teapots from Choson, learned scrolls and strings of coins and rolls of silk from the Ming Empire, spices from the far islands.

In other words, it was the kind of vessel that could take me and the pearl far beyond Madame's grasp and Saiko's revenge. Far beyond anything I had ever known.

NINE

I hunkered down into a gap between two barrels that smelled as if they were full of eels and studied the ship as carefully as a hunter studies his prey.

Barefoot men were rolling barrels up a ramp onto the deck. Others followed them with sacks over their shoulders. A man stood on the jetty, hands behind his back, supervising.

I was no sailor, but this looked to me like a boat readying to cast off.

How many ways would there be to get on board? Hidden inside a sack or a barrel might be a possibility, but a remarkably uncomfortable one. And there would be no way to ensure that I wouldn't end up in the center of a pile belowdecks, to starve or suffocate before I could struggle free.

The sailors were dressed more or less as I was, and there was a chance I might pull my hat low over my face and simply walk on board as one of them. But I hesitated. My time at Madame Chiyome's had taught me many things, and my years with Master Ishikawa had added a few more. How to trim a sail or tie a sailor's knot was not among them. If one of the crew tossed an order my way, I'd be found out in a moment.

Better to wait, then. Wait until the sun was down and I could rely on my old ally the night to do her part. The ramp, no doubt, would be put away once the sailors had finished their work, but there were still the thick ropes that held the ship to the jetty, and they'd be as easy as tree limbs to climb. After that it would simply be a matter of finding somewhere to hide.

I stayed where I was as the afternoon wore away, cupping my hands together and mouthing words of gratitude at the few passersby who tossed a copper coin at me. I must have made quite the piteous spectacle, for someone even dropped a fishtail in my lap, with a few shreds of white flesh still clinging to the bones.

The sun was beginning to settle into a smoky scarlet haze along the horizon when another copper coin fell into my field of vision. I reached up to snatch it as it spun in midair, catching the low sunlight in flashes of ruddy gold, and I saw the sandaled feet of the person who'd thrown it stop in their stride and turn toward me.

I didn't lift my gaze; it would be presumptuous to look someone of higher rank in the face, and everyone was of higher rank than a beggarly cripple like me. But I let the coin fall to my lap in order to free my hands.

The owner of the feet squatted down on his haunches.

"I don't think a feeble beggar would be quite so deft with a coin," Jinnai said. The sun was at his back, casting his face in shadow, but he made no threatening movements and kept his tone friendly and his hands in plain sight. "Other than that, the disguise is very convincing."

I stayed hunched over my pitiful heap of coppers, only narrowing my eyes at him. "What," I said between my teeth, "are you doing here? Otani was supposed to keep you from interfering."

"I've belonged to Master Ishikawa since I was six years old, Kata." I saw his teeth flash in his shadowy face. "There's nothing I can't steal. And there isn't a lock I can't pick or a knot I can't untie. Do you really think some ronin could keep me where I didn't want to be?"

"I kept you tied to a tree all night," I growled.

"Because I let you. Because I wanted to show you that I'm no threat."

"Then go away and leave me alone." I lowered my voice still further, glancing from side to side without moving my head. "You're no threat to me? You're putting me in danger with every word. People are already starting to look at us." I wanted to kick him across the wharf. But I didn't dare. What I'd said was true; people were beginning to glance our way, curious why a handsome young man would stop to chat with a waterside beggar.

"You're not the only one in danger, Kata." He leaned closer, almost as if he meant to kiss me. I tensed. He whispered his next words.

"Your friend Masako? They're going to kill her."

My attention snapped to his face so quickly I saw that he had to keep himself from flinching. I had not thought him capable of easy cruelty, no matter what game he was playing. Had I misread him so badly? Was he actually threatening my friend?

But his face held no menace. And someone else was running along the wharf now—a slight figure in a simple kimono patterned with blue and white diamonds, her sandals slapping the worn wooden boards. She threw herself at me, knocking my hat off. I deliberately turned my muscles to lead to keep my hands from snatching at my knife. The girl knew better than to do that! But she was frantic with worry, and as she clung to me, I put one arm awkwardly around her.

"Kata, you've got to help," she said without taking her face out of my shoulder, her hands gripping fistfuls of my jacket. "They took her. They took her!"

"Who, Ozu?" I got my hands on her shoulders and peeled her away from me so that I could see her face.

"The girls. Fuku. Kazuko. Some others I don't know. They came to the house. She'd just gotten back home."

"They didn't try to take you as well?"

She shook her head, her eyes and cheeks shiny with tears. "They told me to find you. To tell you they'd—they'd kill her—" The pitch of her voice climbed higher and broke. "And the others, too. All of them."

I felt as I had back in the practice yard at the school, when I'd been careless or overconfident and an unexpected blow had gotten under my guard—short of breath, shocked, furious. "All of them?" I repeated.

Aki and Okiko? Yuki? Masako? Every friend I'd asked to help me was now in Madame's clutches?

Ozu plastered her face back against my shoulder and nodded. "If you don't go back to Madame," she said into my jacket. "I told them I didn't know where you were. I told them! But they didn't listen. They just—took her. And Saburro was in the bakery, so he didn't know. It was so quick. But I followed them!"

"You did?" I looked down at her dark head. Ozu had been only seven when I'd bought her and Masako from Madame, bought them both because Masako would not have left without her. So she'd only had the most basic of training. And she'd still managed to follow armed shadow warriors through the streets without getting caught herself? I was impressed. "Where did they take her?"

She sat up straighter and pointed uphill. "To the Takeda mansion."

My heart sank, heavy as the stone anchor that held the ship close to the shore.

"Only I couldn't get in." Ozu wiped her nose on her sleeve. "There's a hedge, and a gate. So I ran back home, because I didn't know where you were, and then—"

"Then I came to the door," Jinnai put in. "The little one remembered me, since I'm a friend of yours." I didn't contradict him, because, as far as Ozu knew, he *was* a friend—she must have met him six days ago when he came to tell Masako that something had happened to me. "And I thought we'd better search for you down by the water," he went on. "Why else would you come back here, after all, if you weren't looking for a boat? So here we all are."

"Kata?" Ozu wiped at her nose again. "You can get Masako back, can't you?"

I looked over her shoulder, at the ship I'd marked out as my likeliest prospect. My old training was tugging at me. I knew what every instructor I'd ever had would have told me, what Madame herself would have told me.

You serve the mission. No one else.

I had a mission, and it was still within my grasp. I was supposed to keep the pearl with me, to keep it unused, and to keep it out of the hands of someone like Kashihara Saiko.

Masako, Aki and Okiko, Yuki—they'd all taken roles in this mission of mine. And if they'd played their roles as they'd been meant to do, no one would have ended up a prisoner. Maybe their skills had been dulled by months or years without a mission. Maybe I'd been wrong to recruit them in the first place.

Regardless, each of them knew that a ninja did not expect help. She did not await rescue.

But were we all still ninjas?

Aki and Okiko were acrobats. Yuki sold her herbs and potions. Masako had married a baker, of all things, and it would not be long, probably, before she'd add her own children to be raised alongside Ozu.

And me? What was I? A thief?

A deadly flower?

If only I could fling the pearl into the ocean, or drop it off a mountainside, and leave it to its fate. But I did not dare. The pearl would not stay lost forever. It was my burden; I could not simply cast it aside. I had to keep it safe. And carrying it into the heart of the Takeda mansion was hardly the way to do that.

If I were faithful to my old training, I should run for that ship and leave my friends to make their own way out of their troubles. If they were faithful to their old training, they'd expect me to do nothing else.

But I'd broken faith with that training two years ago, when Madame had sent me to sink my knife into a boy even younger than I'd been. With frustration tying my guts into knots, I let my gaze fall from the ship to Ozu, sniffling in my arms.

"Go home," I said, and put her back on her feet. I got up myself, pulled my hat low over my face, and started back along the wharf, kicking the pebble out of my sandal and rubbing the bit of gum off of my lip. A filthy waterfront beggar could hardly hope to gain admission to the mansion of the most powerful family of the province.

Ozu was trotting anxiously at my elbow; Jinnai was right behind her. "Kata! Kata, wait! Don't just charge off by yourself," he insisted. "Why won't you listen?"

I spun on him, my impatience steaming over into rage. "Because I already put four friends into danger," I hissed like an angry snake. Then I turned and broke into a run. He might know the waterfront alleys like the lines on his own palm, but give me half a minute's start and we would see if he could keep up with me.

Unfortunately, he could. "Kata, wait! Listen!" I dodged

and weaved between sailors and sail menders, laborers hoisting sacks of rice, fishermen toting baskets of fish. I left the wharf and turned along the muddy road that ran parallel to the water, but I could not seem to leave his voice behind. "Kata, *listen.* You don't—"

And then Jinnai's voice cut off with a startled squawk. I turned just in time to see that a powerful hand had seized the collar of his jacket. It jerked him into a reeking alley between a tavern and a fishmonger's.

I should have kept running. But Ozu had been at Jinnai's heels, and she dove into the alley as well, fierce as a little badger. I groaned and followed. I didn't care much if Jinnai got himself robbed, but if Masako was in a cage somewhere, that made Ozu something like my responsibility.

As it turned out, it wasn't another thief who had tackled Jinnai. From the mouth of the alley, I saw that Otani had one arm tight around Jinnai's neck from behind, and had hoisted him off the ground. His other arm was trying to fend off Ozu, who had apparently appointed herself Jinnai's protector. I snagged the back of the girl's obi before she could launch another kick at the ronin, and held her firmly by the cloth belt for as long as it took for my voice to reach her ears.

"Ozu, stop. He's a friend. Otani, let him breathe." The bandit lowered his captive enough to let the boy's feet touch the ground. All three of them looked at me.

What should I say? How had it happened that the little girl, the ronin, and the thief all seemed to expect me to tell them what to do?

I'd been taught to work alone. My failure to keep that simple rule had left Masako, Aki, Okiko, and Yuki in peril. And here were Ozu, Otani, and Jinnai all waiting for my next word. It was as if I'd acquired a tail that I could not shake off, however much I wanted to.

"I offer my most humble apologies," Otani said into the silence between us. He twisted aside as Jinnai tried to jerk an elbow into his ribs. "Hold still. He's much more slippery than he looks. I'll have him out of the city for you momentarily."

"You can't," Jinnai wheezed, his face gone a dusky red; Otani was letting him breathe, but not much. "Don't give me to him, Kata. You need me. That's what I was trying to tell you."

I needed him? Ridiculous. "Why?" I asked coldly.

"Because," he gasped, "I know where they're keeping your friends."

Ozu shifted in my grasp, ready to launch herself at Otani again. I hesitated, longing for some simple task—a castle wall to climb, a lock to pick, a demon to fight. All of these people, these complications, these uncertainties—it was maddening. How could I know what to choose? How could I know who to trust, if I didn't have the simplest option of trusting no one?

"Let him go," I said wearily to Otani.

The bandit lifted his eyebrows, but loosed his arm and let Jinnai slither to the ground. The thief groaned and staggered to one side to lean against a wall of the tavern, both hands at his throat.

"Say what you know," I told him. "And Ozu, be still. Be

calm. Listen." I looked sternly at her and let go of her obi. "Don't fight unless you can win. You should know that."

"I've been in that mansion," Jinnai said hoarsely, rubbing his throat tenderly and swallowing with a wince. "There was an emerald pendant once, a very attractive design, I must say, and a dagger with a jade handle. There were some scrolls another time, which, I heard, Lord Takeda was very unhappy to have misplaced. I can get you in. If you want your friends back, you're going to have to trust me."

He grinned. I clenched my fists at my side.

I did not trust him. That was out of the question. But did I need him?

Maybe I did.

I could make a plan to get Masako and the others out of a dungeon by myself, I had no doubt of it. If I had a month to do it, and if they had a month to live.

But I didn't have the time, and neither did they.

If Jinnai was right—if he knew the layout of the mansion, knew where prisoners were kept, knew how many guards there would be—then perhaps I could rescue my friends and still get to sea with the pearl on the morning's tide.

My doubt of him was suffocating, but my desire for speed was crushing. Ozu's small, eager face turned up to me, hope flickering behind her eyes like the flame of a lamp in the breeze.

"If you're lying . . . ," I said softly to Jinnai.

His grin faded.

"I've never lied to you once, Kata."

But of course he had—he'd claimed to love me. And that could be nothing but a lie.

I'd heard the songs and listened to the stories that said love was the beauty that burned. A glance over a fan, a whisper behind a screen, a poem dashed across a spotless sheet of rice paper with the flick of a brush.

I'd also seen Masako's husband slap rice flour from his clothes and hair, settle on a mat with a weary grunt, and smile as she knelt to hand him a cup of tea. I'd watched him swing Ozu up into the air until she shrieked with laughter.

Maybe love was one of these things. Maybe something else. But whatever love was, it was not for me.

I was a tool forged for secret battle. The garrote from behind, the poison in the cup, the black blade in the darkness.

A craftsman looked after his tools. A warrior respected his weapons.

But he did not *love* them.

Jinnai had worked at my side long enough to know the truth about me. So why claim love now? He must have known I would not believe him. It could only be some feint in whatever game he was playing, a step toward whatever he hoped to steal from me.

"Not once," he insisted, lying yet again. But it seemed I'd have to trust him anyway, at least long enough to save my oldest friends.

TEN

Otani and I, in another alley between two earthen walls, studied the mansion across the street, or at least what could be seen above the thick hedge that surrounded it. Mostly we were gazing at red roof tiles, glowing in the last of the sunset.

The family who ruled this town and this province spent most of their days in their castle. It was out in the countryside, well walled and defended, far from the perils and pleasures of city life. But every warlord will want to visit his largest town now and then, if only to collect the income from the ships sailing into his harbor or to stop by a temple on the occasion of his youngest son's marriage. And of course he'd need a suitable dwelling.

That dwelling was somewhere behind the hedge. Between the dense wall of bushes and the street there ran a deep ditch, full of water that made the stinking stew of the harbor look clean.

"Keep her out of trouble," I said to Otani. I nodded at Ozu, crouched a few feet away. "And wait for us to come back."

Otani brushed back the hood he'd kept well over his head all the way from the harbor to the city's finest avenue. "If you don't come back, Flower? What then?"

If Jinnai and I found our way into the Takeda mansion, but not back out, I already knew there was no point in asking Otani to come in after us. In the first place, I didn't have the coins left to pay him for a madly dangerous enterprise like that. And in the second, it would have been useless. He was a bandit, and he'd once been a samurai, but since the four of us were not about to charge the place with our swords flashing and arrows humming over our heads, it hardly mattered. He knew nothing of infiltration, of quiet and secret work in the dark. His idea of disguise was a hood over his head. He could not help us even if he wanted to.

"Get her back to her family," I answered. "Masako's husband will look after her." At least I hoped he would, in memory of his wife.

I reached into my belt for another string of coins, but Otani shook his head. "I never fulfilled my first obligation to you," he said quietly, glancing at Jinnai, who was waiting behind me. "This will settle the debt?"

I agreed, rose, and touched Ozu lightly on the shoulder. She looked up, and I wished I had words to offer her anguished, trusting face.

I'd seen that face for the first time the day Ozu had arrived at Madame's school. She'd been nearly five years old, skinny enough to be ugly, with a head of tangles that, in the end, had to be shaved off and a set of lungs that any warrior, bellowing his rage in battle, might have envied.

An aunt had dropped her at the gate, a wizened old peasant woman with next to no flesh on her bones. As a farewell, Ozu bit her. Then she tried to climb the gate. Then she just screamed.

When the tumult had died down, I went to see what I could find out about Madame's newest girl.

Ozu had dug herself a hole under the hedge and was huddled there, refusing to come out, her fierce, wet face peering suspiciously between her grubby knees. Masako was kneeling nearby, talking to her gently. The older girl had the puffy, reddened beginning of an impressive black eye.

When I knelt down as well, Ozu drew in a breath to scream again.

"Make more noise and I'll slice your ears off and put them in the soup tonight," I told her.

Ozu shut her mouth.

Masako glared at me. "No one will hurt you," she told Ozu. "Don't try to scare her, Kata!"

"Don't lie to her." I looked at the little girl in her muddy hole. "That's not much of a hiding place," I offered. "I could show you a better one."

Ozu eyed me skeptically. Masako frowned, got to her feet, pulled me up as well, and dragged me a few paces away.

"What are you doing?" she demanded.

"The same thing you are."

She snorted. "Hardly. You never show any interest in the new girls. What's special about this one?"

I shrugged.

"Let her alone, Kata. She's terrified."

"She fights when she's terrified," I answered.

I'd seen plenty of girls arrive at the school. Some were brought by families who could no longer feed them. Others Madame found by the roadside. Usually they wept, or hid, or fearfully obeyed every command. Very few bit, or punched, or screamed until dust fell from the rafters.

Masako set her face in an expression as stubborn as an ox who wouldn't pull a cart another step. "Don't, Kata."

"Don't what?"

"Don't try to . . ."

I lifted my eyebrows.

"Don't try to make her like you."

I let my breath out slowly through my nose. "You think she's safer being like you?"

"Just let her be. I'll get her out of there."

I shrugged again. It was not worth fighting over a starving scrap of a girl. Let Masako have her, comfort her, look after her, the way she did with all the younger girls. If such coddling ruined what might have been a vicious fighter, what did it matter to me?

"As long as she keeps quiet," I said, and left the two of them together.

Now the same face that had peered out of the hole in the hedge was looking up at me, and I wanted to promise that I'd return safely with the girl who'd been a mother to her. But I could make no such promise.

And if I were too late, or if Masako's prison was too strong, then I would have been right on that day by the hedge. It would have been better for Ozu to learn to be more like me, instead of taking her example from Masako's tender heart.

I flicked a glance at the mouth of the alley, and Ozu dashed off, her muddy sandals slapping the ground. Otani followed her, and a moment or two later, Jinnai and I moved out into the street.

A narrow wooden bridge over the ditch led to a gate in the mansion's hedge, but that was not our destination. Only a fool attacks the enemy's position at its best-defended point. Jinnai led me along the ditch to a corner, and when we turned it we were in an alley even narrower than the first.

On either side was an earthen wall, each higher than my head and topped with a narrow peaked roof to keep off rain and discourage climbers. The Takeda mansion lay to our left, and another estate was to our right, no doubt that of a retainer and ally who'd be delighted to capture a pair of sneaking thieves and hand them over to the city's lord.

Ahead of us, where the alley met another street, I could see Ozu's small form kneeling in the dirt, playing some game with pebbles and sticks. Glancing behind, I saw Otani, hood over his head again, leaning against one of the walls, cleaning his fingernails with his dagger and looking like he might be there all evening.

I turned my gaze back to Jinnai. "You could," I pointed out, "simply tell me about the layout of the place. And the guards. And everything you know."

"I could," he agreed cheerfully, "but I don't want to. Then you'd leave me behind." He'd reached a bamboo pipe protruding through the left-hand wall, dripping an unpleasant ooze into the ditch. Was this his way in? I was not fastidious, but I'd never yet had to crawl through a sewer into a latrine to finish a mission. I'd just as soon not start today.

Jinnai shook his head, as if he'd guessed what I was thinking. "I can manage better than that," he said, and pointed to a second drain, farther down the wall, wider than the first and more pleasant to the nose. All that seemed to be dripping out of it was water.

"The bathhouse drain?"

He nodded. "Follow me."

I'd rather have delayed until full dark, but Jinnai and I had argued this out while we waited for the sun to set. He claimed that, once the light was entirely gone, the guards would begin to patrol the grounds. "Better to make our move early," he'd insisted. "Everyone will have their minds on dinner." Since he knew the territory and I did not, I'd agreed. But it made me nervous all the same.

Now Jinnai looked ahead, to where Ozu knelt, and behind, at Otani. Neither gave any signal of danger, and he seemed satisfied. "Come on."

Without a moment of hesitation, he stepped into the ditch. Mud swallowed his legs up to the calves, but he worked his way across, grabbed the lip of the drain, and heaved himself into it headfirst.

I did hesitate, feeling exposed with the last of the daylight lying across my shoulders. But then I tossed my hat aside and stepped down into the stinking mud as well.

Jinnai was skinny enough to make a good thief, and I was less wide in the shoulders than he was, so I could worm my way into the pipe after him. Not quickly, and not easily. I'd felt exposed before, but that feeling was nothing to letting my backside and legs hang out for all the world to see. Still, I forced myself to trust that Otani and Ozu would keep the alley clear, and at last I wriggled my entire body into the tube.

The pipe seemed to constrict around me. Each breath tightened my ribs and shoulder blades against its surface. I inched forward in darkness, moving up a gentle slope, Jinnai's feet not a handsbreadth from my face, and told myself firmly that of course there was enough air. I was not going to die here, trapped like a rat in a sewer. Like a pebble in a bank of hardened mud. Like a stupid girl who'd trusted a thief.

Each breath tasted stale and damp. I wondered how far we'd gone. I wondered if I could wiggle backward if I needed to, back to that filthy ditch and the free, if foul, air.

Ahead of me, Jinnai's feet stopped moving. I heard a rasping sound, like the chirps from a cricket made of metal, that seemed to go on for several hours, possibly an entire year. Then came Jinnai's whisper.

"Brace my feet."

I squirmed farther up in the pipe. His slimy toes

fumbled at my head. I inched up more so that his feet could rest on my shoulders and tensed myself against the sides of the pipe.

Jinnai pushed. There was a grunt of effort. He pushed harder, and something grated and snapped.

Shoving against my shoulders once more, Jinnai moved forward. It did not take long before his form vanished from the pipe in front of me. Then an arm came groping down, and I seized it and was pulled out.

I gasped for air and wiped damp strands of hair out of my mouth. Crouched beside me, green mildew smeared across his face, Jinnai grinned before he picked up the tiny saw, shorter than his hand, that he'd used to cut through the bamboo slats of the grille covering the drain's mouth. He replaced the saw neatly in a quilted silk bag that he tucked inside his jacket. I glimpsed other tools as well. He came on a mission well prepared.

Two tubs, shoulder height, lurked in the gloom, and buckets were lined neatly against the wall, but there were no signs of bathers or servants. It seemed Jinnai was correct. Everyone, master and mistress and servants alike, was busy with the last meal of the day.

As Jinnai carefully fit the bamboo grille back into place over the mouth of the drain, I stepped off the wooden platform where the tubs and buckets were kept and crossed the smooth earth floor to the bathhouse door. Kneeling, I lowered my head close to the ground, so that my face would not be at eye level, ready to catch the glance of any passerby. Then I slid the door open a crack and peered out.

A formal garden lay ahead of me, dull gray in the fading

light, surrounded by a thick hedge on three sides. On the fourth side, to my left, was a wall of the Takeda mansion. Shadows passed behind screened windows; voices drifted through the paper. Someone was playing a wooden flute indoors, no doubt entertaining the warlord and his guests.

Jinnai came to crouch beside me, studied the garden for a moment or two, slid the door open just enough to squeeze through, and vanished. I went after him.

Only a paper screen separated us from the inhabitants of the mansion at their meal. But at least neither the warlord nor any of his family or friends chose that moment to step outside, slip on their sandals, and take an evening stroll to appreciate the moonlight reflected in the garden's pond.

Still, my back itched as if there were a hundred eyes upon me. I followed Jinnai, sauntering across the smooth stone paths just like an invited guest with every right to be here. We turned and ducked behind the protection of a willow tree dangling its leaves to the ground. Those leaves brushed a hedge with a gate in it, similar to, though smaller than, the one in front of the house.

Jinnai slipped the latch loose and peered through. I joined him.

The last of the light was vanishing, the sky above deepening its shade every minute, stars sharpening from dim sparkles to distinct pinpricks in the blue. And now we were in our keenest danger yet.

We were looking out at a dirt yard where the working buildings of the Takeda residence stood. Directly across from us was a stable with a well nearby. Beside it, a long, low structure that was probably a barracks for soldiers or guards stood against the compound's back wall. On the left side of the yard I glimpsed the kitchen, a small, separate building whose open door let light and heat and smoke spill out. Servants were leaving with full trays and pitchers, returning with empty ones. They seemed to be carrying their burdens into the mansion through a side entrance, rather than crossing their lord's private garden.

The same thing, unfortunately, could not be said of a man who shoved back the door of a latrine alongside the stable's nearest wall, straight in front of us. He stepped out into the quiet night, adjusting the skirts of the short kimono he wore over his full trousers.

The rich brown weave of his clothing was embroidered with maple leaves in red and black; his obi glittered with gold. No servant wore clothes like this. He was a guest or a member of the household, I thought in dismay, as he sighed in relief, stretched, and headed straight across the hard-packed dirt toward us, clearly intending to wander through the garden on his way back to dinner.

I wanted to glare at Jinnai, but he was already burrowing into the roots beneath the hedge, ducking his face against the earth so that only his black hair showed. I eased the gate shut and stepped to the willow tree, slipping through its curtain of leaves, setting the trunk between myself and the intruder.

I pressed my face against the bark, letting my hair blend with the shadows, as Jinnai had done. I could feel my heart thumping against the tree and breathed slowly, easing air in and out between my lips, trying to think of myself as an extension of the willow, living its slow life between root tendril and leaf tip.

Those leaves were still swaying from my passage through them when the garden gate swung open.

Slow breath, slow heartbeat. I didn't dare turn my face to see if Jinnai was well concealed beneath the hedge, to check if the man had noticed a lump beneath the bushes or the restless willow leaves on a night without any wind.

The gate swung shut. Sandals scuffed on the stone path.

The man was humming. With slow, easy steps, he made his way around the pond, passing within arm's reach of the tree where I was hidden. His pace never faltered. I turned my head a fraction of an inch and, through the strands of my hair and the long leaves of the willow, saw him slip off his sandals. In spotless white socks, he stepped onto the veranda. A screen slid open, and warm lamplight streamed out. But all it did was cast deeper shadows over Jinnai and me in our hiding places.

A graceful figure in a long white kimono, hair sweeping smoothly over her shoulders, welcomed the man inside. The screen slid shut.

I stayed still, counted slowly to a hundred, and then peeled myself away from the tree, giving it a soft pat of thanks. Jinnai wriggled out from beneath the hedge.

"I told you we should have waited until they were asleep," I said, with as much venom as I could infuse into my softest whisper.

"And I told you the guards patrol when the family goes

to bed," Jinnai answered as we both came to kneel by the gate once more. "Besides, it wouldn't be half as exciting if everyone was snoring."

My eyes went sharply to his face.

His own eyes were narrow but bright. A smile was tugging at a corner of his mouth. His body was as tense as a bowstring, ready to twang if plucked. His whole face was so vividly alight that I almost didn't need the illumination from the mansion at our backs to see it.

He'd spoken the truth. He was *enjoying* himself. My mission and my friend's lives were at stake, and the partner I'd reluctantly accepted was having fun.

ELEVEN

At the sight of my outraged face, Jinnai only grinned wider.

"Do you think I don't know you, Kata? You wouldn't be half as good if you didn't love this, too," he said under his breath. Then he eased the gate open for a second time.

Servants were still passing back and forth from the kitchen, but fewer now, with longer gaps between them. Jinnai seized one of those gaps to dash through the gate. In a few quick strides he was across the yard, up on the roof of the latrine, then onto the roof of the stable.

I waited, fuming, while a maid moved briskly from the house to the kitchen with an empty pitcher and returned with a full one. How dare Jinnai insult me by claiming I was as reckless as he was?

How dare he know that it wasn't fear or worry for my friends that was quickening my heart, tightening my breath, making my blood rush through my veins until my fingers tingled and twitched?

On my very first mission I'd learned how it felt to be alone in an enemy's stronghold, with nothing but my skills and my silence to guard me from discovery, imprisonment, even torture and death.

It felt like soaring.

It felt cold and sweet as ice.

It felt as if fear itself was sharpened to a tool in my hand.

Every mission was like that. Even this one. Even now. But Jinnai had no right to know it.

Once the maid had disappeared from sight, I took my chance as Jinnai had, charging across the yard, onto the latrine, and up onto the higher roof. I lay flat and rolled over the peak onto the sloping side farthest from the mansion.

Jinnai was there before me. Side by side with him, facedown in the bristly thatch, he and I stretched ourselves out with just our eyes over the roof's highest point. Below, I could hear horses shifting their weight from hoof to hoof. One let out a long, juddering sigh through soft lips.

For the moment, despite my misgivings, Jinnai and I were probably as safe as we could be. If servants or guests or householders passed this way, they were not likely to look up. People rarely did. And even if a restless glance did travel upward, we'd be invisible in the gathering darkness, unless we were fools enough to sit or stand and let ourselves be silhouetted against what little light remained in the sky.

Moving as slowly as a drop of ink soaking into soft paper, I eased myself sideways on the rustling thatch so that my mouth was next to Jinnai's ear. "Plan?" I breathed.

He slowly inched an arm up so that he could tap a

finger on his cheek, near one eye. That finger then moved to point at the yard below us, and I understood his meaning. *Watch. Wait.*

It wasn't much of a plan, but there was nothing better to do.

We lay on the roof while the night settled into the hour of the boar and the horses below us ate and conversed in soft whickers and whinnies. As the animals dined on their hay, insects dined on us. All of the tiny creatures dwelling in the thatch had never enjoyed such a banquet as the two of us offered them.

I set my teeth and did not slap or scratch. Once, Yuki had shown me how the broad, flat leaf of the vanilla plant, crushed and rubbed over the face and hands, kept the worst of the bloodthirsty little beasts at bay. I wished I had some now.

The vanilla plant was not the only one Yuki understood. She knew which leaves, blended into tea, would be the last cup a victim ever drank. Or which roots, dried to powder, would bring an instant slumber, or choke a barking dog, or clot blood in a wound. She'd whisper to her growing things long after she'd stopped talking to Madame, or to the instructors, or to us.

She'd become something like her beloved plants herself, I thought. Silent as a root curling into the soil. Tenacious as a weed.

And hopefully not as dead as hay cut for the threshing, if I could reach her and my other friends in time.

At last a short, stumpy man I assumed must be the cook shut the door of the kitchen for the night. The lights behind the screens in the mansion began to vanish. Then I tensed, and beside me felt Jinnai do the same.

Four men had opened the gate to the garden and were sauntering from the mansion across the yard, their path lit by the paper lantern one carried in his hand. These were not honored guests. I didn't need the rough weave of their jackets and trousers to tell me that. But they were not servants, either. The two swords each wore at his side announced that they were samurais, as did the topknots in their hair and the swagger of each one's gait.

An honor guard, most likely, come with the master to the city to ensure that he and the lady entertaining him were well protected from miscreants like those now on the roof of the stable.

Men responsible for the safety of the household might well look to the rooftops. But if these particular ones were doing so, they were fools to carry a lantern—their vision effectively met a wall where the light failed and the dark began.

Even so, I lay motionless, drawing in only the shallowest of breaths. Something multi-legged explored my hair, and something else bit hard just under my left ear. I thought of ancient stones, fathomless pools, the night sky between the stars, and tried to draw that stillness into my muscles and bones.

The four warriors headed for the barracks. The one with the lantern raised his voice in a song extolling the virtues of the rice wine he'd evidently been drinking, and another shoved at his shoulder and sent him staggering.

It might have turned into a fight, but they seemed too

friendly or perhaps too sleepy to take true offense. They entered the building. Doors slid shut. With tears of relief springing to my eyes, I scratched below my ear.

The last light in the mansion vanished. Jinnai stirred. I grabbed his wrist and gripped tightly to keep him still, feeling the pulse under his skin beat against my fingers.

He froze, almost as if frightened. I let go as though his warm skin were scalding hot.

We waited.

Sounds from the city drifted faintly over the hedges and walls of the estate—a late cart thumping along the rutted road, laughter, an angry bellow, running footsteps, and in the distance, the faint and never-ending rhythm of waves washing the shore and easing back into the depths.

Then a closer sound reached my ear—footsteps.

In a moment I smiled at our good fortune.

The guard patrolling the Takeda estate came wandering by the kitchen, and amazingly, this man was also fool enough to carry his own paper lantern. I heard the faintest whiff of breath leave Jinnai's nose, and I knew he was relieved and amused as well.

The man was lazy, too. He glanced briefly inside the formal gardens, shut the gate again, wandered the length of the stables (humming under his breath as he did so), leaned on the well for several long minutes, strolled past the kitchen again, and disappeared around a corner of the house.

He didn't come back.

Without the distraction of his lantern, my night vision sharpened. I couldn't see details, but the shapes of buildings steadied and took on a more distinct edge. All was darkness, but the darkness of walls and roofs was deeper and more solid than that of grass or dirt or sky. I could move where I needed to now, within the compound, and I would not put a foot wrong or walk into a building or fall into the well.

Jinnai evidently felt the same, for he rose cautiously to his hands and knees. The thatch rustled under his weight, and under mine as I did the same. To my oversensitive ears, we sounded like badgers crashing through a thicket, but nothing and no one in the compound stirred.

Jinnai crawled to the edge of the stable roof, where he crouched. Then he jumped.

He landed neatly and accurately on the roof of the samurais' barracks. He froze. Could they have missed the sound? The rooftop was still safer than the ground; if that guard came back on his rounds, we'd only have to drop facedown to be invisible once again. Even so, the noise made me wince. Now Jinnai was a bear, not a badger.

I shifted my weight and flexed my knees and shoulders and back, stiff from lying still for so long. Then I followed Jinnai to the edge and jumped as well.

I tried to land softly, letting feet, knees, and hands all take some weight, but still . . . noise was unavoidable. Only thick straw and rafters and a few feet of space separated us from sleeping men with weapons close at hand. At least I hoped they were still sleeping.

I ached to ask Jinnai where he was leading me—to trail behind him like a child holding her mother's kimono irritated every one of my instincts. But I didn't dare add words to the noise of our passage. Barefoot, his sandals slung across his shoulder, Jinnai walked the length of the barracks. I kept a few feet behind, to distribute our weight more widely. All we needed was for a foot to poke through the thatch right over the nose of a sleeping samurai.

At the end of the barracks, as far as possible from the stable, Jinnai paused and crouched, waiting for me to catch up. When I did, he pointed down.

I crawled beside him. "They're here?"

He nodded.

"Door?"

"Inside."

So the barracks had a cell for keeping prisoners, and the door to that cell was located inside the building. No chance that one of us could simply pick the lock to let Masako and the others out.

The walls were cedar and sturdy. Jinnai's little saw would be no use here. That left the roof—with thatch a foot thick and solid rafters beneath—or the floor.

"Watch for the guard," I said, shaping each word carefully so it was barely louder than a breath. "If you see him, be an owl."

I felt his nod more than I saw it.

Then I crawled to the roof's edge, lowered myself to hang by my hands, and dropped lightly down.

A narrow veranda ran along one edge of the barracks, and from it thin slats of wood extended to the ground. They were for show, not support, and broke easily under my hand.

I'd cleared a space as wide as my shoulders when Jinnai's soft owl call came from above. I could have vaulted back up on the roof, but that might have been noisy. Instead I wormed as quickly and quietly as I could through the hole I had made and burrowed into the cool space beneath the barracks' floor.

The gap between the bamboo floor above me and the damp earth below was, perhaps, two feet—not enough to sit up, but fairly roomy as long as I lay flat. The darkness all around me now was not friendly, as it had been outside. It was thick and humid and stifling, like a wet cloth over the face, and offered no texture to the eye.

There was light outside, though. Through the broken slats, I saw the guard's lantern glimmer and advance. The wood of the veranda creaked and the floor above my head gave slightly as the man settled down for a rest.

He was sitting directly above me. How long would he stay there?

I counted. By the time I'd reached five hundred, he'd started to hum a tune.

I began counting at one again and had only reached twenty when the guard's music cut off. His breath whooshed out and the wood of the veranda creaked again as if its load had lightened.

Something limp and heavy fell to the grass outside, and a moment later, Jinnai squirmed through the gap I'd made with the guard's glowing lantern in his hand.

Blinking and dazzled, my night vision vanished like a dream upon waking, I clenched my teeth to keep the curse that exploded in my mind from bursting out of my mouth. He'd killed the guard? Or knocked him out? We could have waited. We *should* have waited. The man could not have sat there forever, and now we had a body lying in the dirt—an obvious sign to anyone who happened to look that something was wrong.

Jinnai was not soaring on the thrill of a mission now; he was coasting on luck. And luck is a dreadful, deceitful ally.

I could not scream this truth into the reckless boy's ear, not with sleeping samurai a few feet over our heads. But oh, if I ever took *anyone* along on a mission again . . .

When at last I'd tamed my frustration to a whisper, I let it out. "Are you mad? Someone will see!"

"No one to see," Jinnai muttered. All the same, he pulled his wide cloth belt loose and wrapped it around the lantern, dimming its light. I added my own obi, and between the two of us, we muffled the lantern until only a sliver of light fell onto the bamboo slats of the floor above us.

I still didn't like it. Even with the light controlled, it might draw attention. It had already ruined our eyes for the dark outside. If we needed to react to a threat, we'd be at a disadvantage.

But it would make things quicker.

Speed is essential. Hurry is perilous.

A lantern was hurry, not speed. But perhaps we needed it. The hour of the rat was probably upon us, and we still had to crack open this prison, get the girls out, and find our way once more over the mansion's walls.

On my back, I squirmed deeper beneath the building and set the tip of my knife to a knot I'd found in the floorboards. As I'd hoped, they were made of bamboo and fairly thin; Jinnai's little saw would serve. I pried at the knot and it popped neatly out, leaving a hole about the size of my eye.

I wriggled aside, and Jinnai applied his miniature saw to the opening.

We took turns holding the lantern and wielding the saw. It was slow, awkward work. Soon my hands ached and a small, vicious spot of pain danced between my shoulder blades. Sawdust drifted down into our eyes and up our noses. When I nicked my thumb, blood began a slow trickle along my arm.

And the light did draw attention, just as I had feared. Moths came fluttering beneath the veranda, like tiny, clinging scraps of grayish-brown silk, brushing their powdery wings across our faces. Worms squirmed in the dirt beneath us; beetles scuttled out of our way. Once a centipede crawled up my sleeve as I was steadily sawing, tiny claws clinging to the cloth. I didn't notice it until it nearly reached my wrist, and then I left the saw sticking in the floorboards so that I could flail my arm and send the vile thing flying.

I *hate* centipedes.

Ignoring Jinnai's incredulous stare, I settled back down to the work. We had the hole about a handspan wide when a voice, low and hoarse, came from above. "Kata?"

I paused in the sawing, feeling warm relief lick along my bones. Jinnai had been a guide worth following. The voice was Masako's.

"It's me," I answered, my voice low as well. There was no way to explain Jinnai's presence to her now; that would have to come later. "Are the others there?"

Masako had stretched herself flat on the floor beside the hole; I could feel her weight on the boards above me. After a brief pause, during which I could nearly sense her astonishment soaking through the bamboo slats, she spoke again.

"We're all here. Pass the saw up. It will be easier."

I did so. Jinnai directed the light, and we saw the small, toothed blade flash steadily in and out of the wood. One floorboard after another cracked and broke, and at last, Masako slid feetfirst through the opening we had created.

She looked at me and shook her head, blinking, her eyes bright with tears. I frowned. Emotion had no place on a mission; she knew that. Gratitude, relief, astonishment—those were for later.

Lithe as lizards, Aki and Okiko eased through the opening, and we squirmed aside to make room for them. Yuki was last, and once she had joined us, Jinnai pulled our cloth belts from the paper lantern, tossed mine back to me, and blew out the flame.

Darkness swooped in around us. All I could rely on to guide me was touch and the faint hint of fresher air from the opening I'd made under the veranda.

There was a confused moment or two. Someone's elbow hit my ear; a knee pushed into my back. Then we seemed to have sorted out which way to move. There was more space around me, and I heard a grunt of effort as cloth rubbed on wood. Someone had made it through our gap under the veranda—Jinnai, probably, since he knew where it was.

Masako was beside me. I tugged her in the right direction and then patted her to tell her to stay still. I wormed out of the hole myself before reaching back in to pull at Masako's sleeve, letting her know it was her turn.

My night vision began to trickle back. Overhead, a half-moon gave enough light to turn packed earth a paler shade of gray than grass, to distinguish between the prickly denseness of a hedge and smooth wooden walls, and to show me where the guard's body lay, unmoving but still breathing, beside the veranda. I reached out a hand to touch Jinnai on my left, the soft cotton of his sleeve, the firm arm beneath it.

Something squirmed onto my feet, and I leaned down to help Masako up. The other girls came after her.

I was helping Yuki rise when I heard Jinnai draw in a quick breath.

Figures stepped away from the hedge, from beneath the stable's overhanging roof. One straightened up from crouching behind the well. Another dropped from the barracks' roof to land as lightly as a tengu on the ground.

It was as if they'd sculpted themselves out of the night, and for half a moment I thought we were facing ghosts. No, that couldn't be—I heard footfalls on the earth, as soft as a brush, heavy with ink, stroking paper. And ghosts, as everyone knows, have no feet.

I heard a familiar sound, metal against metal, and light sprang out of a dark lantern that one figure held in her hand. She turned the lantern's cover to direct the light where she wanted it to go.

My knife was in my hand, and I threw it as hard as I could straight at the source of the light that lanced across the yard, pinning the six of us with its brilliance. In darkness, we could scatter, try to find cover. Perhaps some of us could make it over the wall. In darkness, we still had a sliver of a chance.

A second thrown knife whirled out of the night, hitting mine perfectly, knocking both weapons harmlessly to the ground.

The hand holding the lantern never wavered.

"I knew you would make it this far," Madame Chiyome said, the faintest expression of satisfaction on her face as she looked over the lantern at me. "I knew I trained you well enough for that."

Around Madame Chiyome, in the edge of the light, I saw Kazuko and Oichi with their bows at full draw, and three girls I did not know with blades at their sides and throwing knives at the ready. Madame herself seemed to be unarmed, but that was not to be trusted. Besides, she had five fully trained ninjas at her command—they were her blades, her shield, her arrows. Tempered to a fierce strength, honed to a deadly sharpness.

Without a word, Madame turned and gestured with a graceful arm toward the mansion. The sleeve of her kimono, a blue as deep as the sea at dusk, rippled through the air.

I started toward the house, my friends close behind, the ring of armed girls alert to our every move.

TWELVE

Kazuko slid open one of the wooden shutters and the paper screen behind it. Madame stepped inside, leaving her sandals on the ground. I did the same. I might be filthy, covered with mud and slime from a bath drain, bug-bitten, disheveled, and defeated, but I was not a barbarian, to wear my shoes indoors.

A question nagged at me as I followed my captors through an empty room. Where was Fuku? She'd been in charge of the first mission to apprehend me. Had Madame dismissed her in disgrace for her failure? Punished her? Or was she here, somewhere that I could not see?

The thought made my skin twitch. A scorpion in the middle of an otherwise empty mat is much less deadly than one hiding in your sock.

The second question swirling inside my brain was: Had Jinnai planned what had just happened?

Perhaps not. Perhaps he had been as surprised as I was

when several shadow warriors stepped out of the night. Yet I could not avoid the thought. I'd followed him right to the place where Madame had sprung her trap. And the thought had a companion: If Jinnai had not tracked me through the woods, I would not be here now.

He was behind me, silent, so I could not scan his face for shock or guilt or triumph. Still, doubt wormed into my mind. To trust a thief had been a weak and foolish error.

To come back for Masako and the others had been a worse one.

I might have been hidden on a ship right now. I and the pearl in my pocket could be out to sea, vanished from this city like smoke from a lamp, like a ghost in sunlight.

If I'd followed my training, kicked Jinnai into the harbor, ignored Ozu's tears, left my friends to their fate, then I'd be safe.

The pearl would be safe.

I would have been faithful to my mission.

Instead, I was a prisoner. My friends were still prisoners. I'd accomplished nothing. In fact, I'd made things worse.

Ahead of me, Madame slid open another screen. She led us into a short corridor. There, while Oichi kept her bow drawn, Kazuko searched me quickly and expertly. Soon the garrote from around my waist, the blade inside my hair ornament, lockpicks and pry bars were in a pile on the matting.

Jinnai was treated the same way. His array of sharp, useful, and deadly objects was even more impressive than mine. Masako and the other girls, of course, had nothing but their clothing.

I expected Madame to confiscate the pearl as well, but she did not. Well, that made sense. She knew that I had it; she would leave it to Saiko to take it from me.

Or from my corpse.

As one of the girls I did not know slid open a screen, I slipped a hand inside my pocket to touch the pearl, perhaps for the last time. Before I'd even tied the pocket shut, Madame stepped through the door and we all followed her into the mansion's large, central chamber. A third question billowed up in my mind, taking up all the space there.

How exactly would Saiko kill me?

She was standing before a painted screen that stretched from floor to ceiling and showed a slim tree in snowy bloom against a golden background. The precious metal seemed to multiply the light of the two paper lanterns on the floor beside her, and against that background, Saiko, in her kimono of ivory silk with an obi of pale pink, her soft hair loose over her shoulders, looked very much like a branch of flowering cherry herself.

She held out one soft hand to me. What did Kashihara Saiko's hands tell me about her soul?

Smooth and pale, every nail polished until it gleamed, every finger curled in graceful anticipation that what she wanted would be given to her, Saiko's hands were as perfect as the rest of her. And as deceitful. They showed no flaw.

Then I saw that her hand, ever so slightly, was trembling.

Her face, expressionless as a seashell, told me nothing. With her eyebrows plucked and repainted in graceful arcs, her lips reddened with safflower, her skin lightened with rice powder, she looked nothing but elegant. It was hard to believe I'd ever seen her dressed like a peasant, dusty from the road, bedraggled from days of struggling through mountains. It was even harder to believe I'd ever protected her or fought demons by her side. Or thought, however briefly, of trusting her.

Still, as perfect as she was, she couldn't stop her hand from shaking. Jinnai might be a liar, but he'd been right about this. Saiko's greed, her ambition, her hunger for revenge, all showed in her trembling hand.

"You have something that belongs to me," she said.

As if to bring into my mind everyone I'd ever trusted foolishly, Jinnai, entering the room last, tripped on the edge of a mat and stumbled, grabbing at me to keep himself upright. He practically climbed up me as if I were a tree. Impatiently, I thrust him off, keeping my eyes warily on Saiko.

I shook my head.

Saiko's hand sank slowly to her side.

"How much choice do you think you have, Kata?" Jinnai and the other girls might as well have been invisible to Saiko; she didn't look away from my face. "You can choose to give me the pearl before your death, or after."

"If you kill me, you can't take it from me," I pointed out, letting a taunt slip into my voice, as if her stupidity amused me. "Anyone else could take it from my body. They could pick it up from the dust of the road, if they found it, and wish on it. But you never could."

"You know I know that." The faintest flicker of impatience crossed her face, which meant a bubbling volcano of rage was concealed within. "It's mine. It has belonged to my family for generations. I know the rules that govern it far better than you do. And there are plenty of hands here to wield a knife."

True enough . . .

I let my gaze move away from Saiko to scan my surroundings. The screen we had used to enter the room was behind me. I knew without looking that exit would be guarded. There were four more doors to the room, and one armed girl stood in front of each.

"If you kill me here, it will be messy. And loud," I countered. One side of the room had a wall of windows, each covered now by its wooden shutter. I wouldn't have time to open one before there would be a knife or an arrow in my back. "The Takeda family might be disturbed," I went on. "How will you explain a corpse in their mansion? Blood all over their clean floor mats?"

I had no weapons. But there were those two lanterns burning on the floor. And straw mats catch a blaze quickly.

Saiko smiled gently. "The only one of the Takeda family here tonight is my new husband. And he's sleeping very soundly. I made sure of that."

Husband? I had been talking idly, using my words as if they were smoke I could blow in Saiko's eyes while my own eyes and mind were busy trying to find an escape. But this word snapped my attention back to her.

Her slight smile stayed in place as if carved on her lips. "Didn't you hear? I married Takeda Narikazu less than a month ago. He has two older brothers, of course, but that shouldn't be . . . permanent."

How would she assassinate her new brothers-in-law, I wondered. Poison? Accident? A fall down a well? An attack by bandits? There were so many ways she could ensure her husband would end up the sole heir of his powerful family. Would he even know what his charming new wife was doing?

"I think we've spent enough time on pleasantries now." She held out her hand once more, the sleeve of her kimono swaying to reveal the under robes beneath—pale green, blood crimson, soft blue.

"I agree." Okiko's voice, sudden and firm, startled everyone. As I jerked my head around to look at her, she whirled and launched a perfect kick that connected with the back of her sister's head.

Aki fell to the floor mats and lay motionless. Masako cried out and stepped forward, only to freeze as arrows swiveled to point at her.

I kept my feet still, but shock clamped down on my lungs and forced all the air out. For a moment I was back in the practice yard at the school, feeling packed dirt beneath my feet, the smell of dust and sweat in my nostrils.

Madame's rule had been that every student of an age to fight must face every other. No exceptions were made for size or skill or years of training. We all fought each other every day.

Except for Aki and Okiko.

It was the only time in twelve years that I'd seen Madame's methods fail. No punishment she could come up with—and Madame was inventive in her punishments—

could force either twin to attack the other.

And now, Okiko had struck her sister down? I felt as if I'd seen someone's hand attack her own arm.

"You told me we could go free," Okiko said to Saiko, firmly ignoring everyone else in the room. "Once you had Kata, you'd let us go. She's here. I want what you promised."

"Okiko," Masako whispered, her face stricken. "You told them?"

Saiko waved a pale, smooth hand at Okiko, without a flicker of interest on her face. Okiko knelt down by Aki's body.

"You told her where to find us?" Masako went on, as if her words could create belief in her own mind. "I couldn't understand how easily they captured all of us. It was you?"

Okiko shrugged without looking up. "How long do you think you would have stayed free, Masako?" she asked impatiently. "Four girls against Madame Chiyome, and the Takeda family, *and* the Kashiharas? It was madness all along. I was willing to pay off my debt, but not to commit suicide for Kata. Or to let my sister do the same."

She spoke only to Masako. She didn't look at me. But I had something to say to her.

"You betrayed the mission," I said flatly, and she flinched as if a bamboo rod had landed across her back. Still, she didn't turn her eyes my way.

"I saved my sister," she answered, and bent to heave Aki's limp body up over her shoulders.

"And what will she think when she wakes up?" Masako asked. "Okiko, she'll never forgive you."

Okiko straightened with a grunt.

"But she'll be alive to hate me," she answered, and she carried Aki out of the room. Oichi stood aside, letting her open a screen, then closing it behind her.

"Now," Saiko said, as if the interlude with Okiko had been nothing more than a minor nuisance. "Give the pearl to me, or I'll take it from your body."

I didn't have time. Didn't have time to absorb the knowledge that Okiko had chosen to repay her debt with betrayal.

"Kazuko?" Masako said softly. "Oichi?"

Kazuko's gaze did not falter when Masako said her name. Neither did her hand on her bowstring. Oichi's arrow was aimed straight at my head. Masako was a fool to think, even for a moment, that an appeal to their hearts might have been effective when they had a mission to perform.

I'd been a worse fool to think anyone but myself could serve my mission. That had gotten me into this mess. But I could still get myself out of it.

I could wish.

At the thought, a soft, gleeful, malicious chuckle echoed inside my head.

There might be two wishes left for the pearl. There might be only one. Could it truly be that Saiko had not thought of this? Did she think she was watching me so carefully that I'd die before a wish had passed my lips? Didn't she know a desire could simply form inside my mind?

If I wished now, I could get the pearl away from here. I could get myself and Masako and Yuki to safety—at the cost, perhaps, of my own soul.

"Take it. Here it is."

When Okiko had spoken up, it had surprised me. But when Jinnai did the same, it seemed to stop my heart for a beat.

Lazily, as if it were of no great consequence, Jinnai tossed the pearl through the air to Saiko.

It spun like a tiny moon, white and gold. But just as the real moon is marked by blotches of shadow, so the pearl was marked by stains of dull, rust red.

I'd nicked my thumb on the blade of Jinnai's saw. I'd reached inside my jacket to touch the pearl. My blood was on it—so now it only needed my word to transfer the pearl and its demon to a new master.

Saiko's hand snaked out to snatch the pearl. Mine slapped against my flat and empty pocket. Jinnai had been right—there was no pocket he couldn't pick.

"It's not worth your life, Kata," Jinnai said. "No matter what it is. Don't look at me like that. There's always more treasure to steal."

My heartbeat thundered back at full force, and my hands tightened into fists that felt as if they would never unclench. Okiko's treachery had only shocked me, but for some reason I could not identify, Jinnai's filled me with instant, murderous rage.

Emotions had no place on a mission. I would certainly deal with the thief later, but for now, my full attention had to be on Saiko and her slowly widening smile.

"I wish . . . ," she said aloud, softly, tightening her fingers around the pearl.

Nothing happened. Not a thing in the room changed.

"It can't be stolen," I said. All the others in the room—Masako, Jinnai, Madame, the rest of the girls—felt as remote as those distant lands and coasts on Master Ishikawa's map.

The pearl burned in Saiko's hand, and its power bound the two of us as tightly together as muscle is bound to bone.

"As long as I'm alive, it must be given," I continued. "He doesn't know the rules." I flicked a contemptuous glance at Jinnai. "But I thought you did."

And I wished. Better to spend my soul than leave the pearl to Saiko.

Take me far from here. Masako and Yuki, too. Now that Jinnai had proved himself a traitor, I would happily leave him to his fate. *Over the mountains, across the sea—I don't care. Now.*

Again that evil laugh made the hairs on the back of my neck stir. Only I could hear it. Or did it echo inside Saiko's head as well as mine?

Ah, little one, you're too far away. Why not speak the words and give me to this other? Her soul is not quite as entertaining as yours, but it's been so long . . . and I am so hungry . . .

I couldn't wish, either. The pearl would not serve either of us.

Saiko's smile faded.

"This changes nothing," she said, and flicked her fingers at Kazuko. "Once you're dead, anyone can take it—and I'm the one who has it."

"Not if I give it away before I die," I countered, suddenly seeing my next move in our game. I could name a new owner of the pearl even while it was in Saiko's hand. All that was needed was my blood, already on its surface, and my will. I knew it would work, because it was what Saiko's father had done, years ago, to leave the pearl to his son.

I'd been meant to kill that son, Saiko's little brother, and I had ended up saving him. Panicked for his life, Ichiro had pressed the bloodied pearl into my hand and told me it was mine.

I could reverse that process now. I could give the pearl back. Safe in his monastery over the mountains, guarded by warrior monks who could face down samurai, Ichiro could become the jewel's guardian once again, and Saiko would still be powerless.

I drew a breath, ready to speak the words, and Saiko's eyes widened with alarm. She pointed, and the tip of Kazuko's arrow swung away from my head toward Jinnai's heart. "Say it and watch him die," she snapped.

Like a fool, I hesitated.

"Ah." Jinnai looked from the tip of Kazuko's arrow to Saiko's face to me. "Kata, perhaps you're not entirely happy with what I just did, but—"

"Not in the heart," Saiko said to Kazuko. "Somewhere . . . less quiet. More painful."

"—really, I wanted to help. I did. Kata?"

"You could shoot him in the knee first," I suggested to Kazuko. "That might be a good start."

Jinnai winced. But Saiko lifted her hand once more, and Kazuko lowered her bow again.

"So you don't care about this boy," Saiko said. "Such a pity. He likes you so much. But maybe there's another way."

There was no smile on her face now. "Say it's mine, Kata. It always has been rightfully so. And there is someone I know you care about." Her gaze went to Masako, but she shook her head. "If you don't give me the pearl, I'll make sure Ichiro dies."

Ichiro? My plan began to crumble like cracked pottery, and Saiko's entire face softened with pleasure.

"He came to celebrate my marriage, of course," she went on. "He's sleeping in the room next door. Fuku is there with him. Just as you were, two years ago. But Fuku doesn't have your tender heart."

She laughed delicately at the look I could feel sliding across my face.

"I don't have your tender heart, either, Kata," she told me. "Do you know what happened in your old province since you stole the pearl from my family? My uncle could not defend his borders without its power. He lost land, and taxes, and influence, until the best marriage bargain he could make for me was a drunken weakling. You here on the coast, Ichiro safe in his monastery—did either of you even know what was happening to the Kashiharas? How weak we've become? How helpless? How *poor*?" Disgust made the last word snap like a lash.

"Say the pearl is mine, or she'll kill him. Don't stop to think. I won't give you time. You can't win now, not against me, not against all I can do to you. Say it now, or he dies."

She'd told me not to think, but I could not stop thoughts from stampeding through my mind.

The girl I'd known two years ago had been clever,

ruthless, devious, and eager for power. But she'd disrupted my first mission to save her brother's life.

Would she truly have him killed now?

She would.

She would do so happily, I realized, with a chill as great as if I'd stepped on ice and it had given way beneath me, dumping me over my head into the freezing water beneath. She'd kill her own brother to become the owner of the pearl. In fact, she would sooner kill him than me, because then I'd still be here to know that a boy I'd kept alive at considerable trouble—a boy who'd come to be my friend—was dead.

I'd tricked Saiko two years ago, leaving her holding a polished white pebble while I escaped with her family heirloom, and she could not stand that. She'd kill Jinnai—Masako—Ichiro—anyone but me. She needed to keep me alive, to let me know she'd won.

All those thoughts spun through my head in the time it took to draw a breath. I opened my mouth to speak.

But before the first word could leave my lips, Fuku came flying through a screen, shredding paper and splintering wood. She hit the ground hard, rolled once, and lay sprawled at Saiko's feet.

Someone stepped through the shattered screen after her. He glanced around the room, tucked his staff under one arm, put his hands together, and bowed.

"Kata," he said politely. "Masako. Elder sister."

THIRTEEN

Ichiro was wearing the loose white under robe of a monk. His hair was in a novice's topknot. And that was not the only change. He was taller and heavier, and all of the additional weight looked like muscle. He gazed at the sister who'd been planning his death with no shock, no grief, no rage on his face.

"You said Kata could not win," he said. "But it's you, elder sister. You can't hope to win."

"You could kill Kata," Masako said, stepping to my side. "Perhaps. You might kill all of us. But we have friends outside this room. And one of them will find you. Any servant, any merchant, any singer or dancer, any cook or washerwoman who steps into this house might actually be one of us. You would never be safe. You can let us all go now, or you can live your life alone and afraid of every footfall, every shadow on a screen."

Saiko whirled to Madame, who all this time had been

standing silent with her back against a wall, listening and observing.

I felt my heart tighten.

All the time I'd been feinting and sparring and struggling with Saiko for the upper hand, Madame had been at my back. I might be a match for Saiko; I'd bested her before, if only barely. But Madame?

Madame's gaze went coolly from Saiko to me. Then it flickered over the others—Masako, Yuki, even Jinnai—before she returned her attention to me. She looked as if she were adding up numbers in her head.

She was calculating odds, I realized. I'd seen that look on her face as she watched two girls sparring in the practice yard, quietly predicting who would win.

Could she be making up her mind which of us—Saiko or me—was likelier to leave this room alive? Was she considering who she'd prefer to have on her side once this night was over? And who would be more dangerous as an enemy?

Madame lifted her hand and let it fall. Instantly, Kazuko and Oichi lowered their bows, the strings slackening. The other ninjas sheathed their blades.

Saiko opened her mouth to protest, but Madame's words came first.

"I fulfilled my contract with you when I brought Kata into this room," she said, her voice dry and precise. "You failed to deal with her. That is not my concern."

Panic overtook Saiko's rage. Her gaze moved from her brother in his monk's robe, to the dark-clad girls with their lowered weapons, to my face.

"If I scream, guards will be here in a moment," Saiko threatened. "You can't—you wouldn't dare—"

Masako laid a gentle hand on my arm.

"We're leaving now," she said, to me or Saiko; I could not tell which.

But the pearl. The pearl was still in Saiko's hand. How could I leave her with it? It was my burden, my responsibility, my mission. No one else's. Mine.

Jinnai grabbed my other arm.

"There's always more to steal," he insisted. Of course this fool of a thief didn't know—he couldn't know—the true value, or the true power, of what he'd lifted so cleverly from my pocket.

"*Always,*" he said, almost impatiently, his voice so low that it reached my ears only.

Ichiro closed in behind, Yuki at his side. The four of them herded me out of the room.

Before I went, I had a last glimpse over my shoulder of Saiko. Beautiful. Furious. Her hand went up to rub her face, smearing ink from her painted eyebrows across her forehead. She looked like a ghost I had once met, forever hungry for what she could not have.

Then Jinnai pulled me away. Screens slid open and shut. There was a garden, a gate in a thick hedge, a street, and Ozu tight in Masako's arms.

I would have dealt with Jinnai there and then, but Masako was insisting that it was too dangerous to stay where we were, Ichiro was agreeing with her, and Otani had loomed up in front of me, threatening to throw me over his shoulder if I did not move. Before I could shake off the thick fog of failure that was blinding and choking me, we were in an alley off the main avenue, cramped between two buildings, and Jinnai was backing away from the look on my face.

"You," I said, my voice low and savage.

"Kata, listen—"

My anger was a flower blossoming inside me, its roots deep in my gut, its petals spreading inside my rib cage, enclosing my heart.

Wasn't that what I was, what I'd been trained to be? A deadly flower?

"You took the pearl from me," I told him, advancing step by step.

Masako moved as if to get between us, but Otani shook his head, and she was still.

"I was trying to—," Jinnai spluttered.

"What kind of a fool was I? To trust you?" I growled.

To trust all of them? To trust any of them?

First Okiko, then Jinnai. Who next? It was like running up a staircase at full tilt, not knowing which tread would dissolve beneath my foot. And the worst of my scalding anger was for myself.

Trust no friend farther than you can see her. Trust no ally for more than you've paid him.

What a fool I was to have forgotten. What a fool they'd made me.

Okiko was gone. I could hardly attack myself. But

Jinnai was still in range, and what he'd done was the least forgivable. Okiko had handed me over to Madame, but Jinnai had handed the pearl over to Saiko.

My weapons were inside the Takeda mansion, but that did not mean I was helpless. My anger burst into action. Jinnai stumbled farther back, his hands up to protect his face, his jumbled words of protest barely reaching my ears. Blood dripped from a cut over his eyebrow after my first blow landed. Before I could launch a second, he was gone, footsteps fading into the darkness all around.

I would have pursued him, but Ichiro gripped my shoulder. I threw his hand off.

"Revenge is like drinking vinegar when you're dying of thirst," he said softly.

"Oh?" I turned on him, my nerves still bristling with the urge to hit something, kick someone, attack an enemy I could actually see. "So you'd forgive your sister, then? Pour her a cup of tea? Say a prayer for her?"

"Well, I won't be accepting any more wedding invitations from her," Ichiro said mildly. "But I wouldn't chase her down a dark alley, either."

Otani coughed into his fist.

"You sound just like Tosabo," I told Ichiro, my words snapping at the air like little whips, even while the flower of rage inside me began to wilt. "Is that what you've been learning in your monastery?"

Ichiro shrugged. "That, and how to kick someone through a screen."

Otani snorted. A corner of Yuki's mouth twitched. I

sighed and let the tension in my muscles ebb. Why was I so enraged, after all? Hadn't I always believed that Jinnai would steal what he wanted whenever he could?

"It isn't as bad as you think, Kata," Masako reminded me. "Saiko can't use the pearl."

"If I die, she can," I pointed out.

"I don't quite know all the details of what's happening," Otani said. "But it seems that our next step must be to keep you alive, Flower. The street might not be the safest place to discuss that. I think I know somewhere we might go."

※　※　※

When we entered the wineshop Otani had in mind, I noticed that the ronin caught the owner's eye. The place was so small that the entryway and the kitchen were one and the same, and the man rose from where he was kneeling before a stove, stirring the fire inside, to greet us. I saw coins slip from Otani's fingers to his.

The owner tucked the payment into his belt and just as quickly gestured us to step up on the wooden platform to our right. Those of us who still wore our sandals left them there, alongside others, and we entered the shop's main (and only) room.

Surely it was the hour of the tiger by now, and dawn could not be far away. A place open at this time of night was not likely to have the finest clientele. Only a few determined drinkers were still here—a group of three men throwing dice in one corner, a slumped and solitary figure dozing in another. Otani led us to the back of the room, where he used a toe to nudge a snoring cat off one of the flat and filthy cushions on the ragged mats.

Beside us was a window, several of its paper panes torn and the rest smudged with dirt. Through the ragged bits of paper, I could glimpse the river, an oily blackness uncoiling endlessly alongside the building, and a half-rotted dock that led right to the back door. Handy for loading wine barrels and perhaps unloading customers who had the poor judgment to cause trouble—or to have purses that looked too heavy.

After the briefest of glances, the three men in the corner had returned to their game, ignoring us. This wasn't the sort of establishment where it paid to show too much interest in your neighbors.

Without being asked, the owner brought over a low table and returned to slap none-too-clean cups full of rice wine down on its surface. "Something to eat, too, Shiburo," Otani told him. The man grunted and came back with bowls of soup. The broth was thin and greasy, but it still held the salty tang of miso. As its warmth reached my stomach, the hard knots there began to loosen.

"Shiburo knows me," Otani said in a low voice. "And he'll keep it quiet that we were here."

"You trust him?" I asked, cradling my soup bowl in my hands.

Trust no friend. Trust no ally.

Otani snorted. "I've made it well worth his while to be trustworthy. So, Flower, what are we to do next?"

I had no answer for him.

I'd thought my old instructors, back at Madame's

school, had always taught me to rely on myself because no help would come. *A foot soldier has his unit. A samurai has his comrades. A warlord has his retainers. A ninja has no one.*

But there was more to it than that, I realized now. A ninja was alone—or should be alone—because friendship, alliance, even something as absurd as love, would take her loyalty away from her mission.

"She has to leave this city," Masako said quickly. She had an arm around Ozu, who pressed close to her side, wide-eyed and alert but silent.

Given a choice between my mission and her sister, Okiko had chosen Aki. I could have predicted that, if I'd paused for thought.

"Not just the city," Ichiro chimed in. "The province, too. You must protect yourself now."

Yuki nodded.

Otani had his men, the bandits who'd sworn him loyalty when they'd been his soldiers and had not withdrawn it when he'd become an outlaw. Masako had Ozu and that husband of hers. Ichiro had so many ties now—his master, Tosabo; the abbot of his monastery; his fellow monks. And Yuki? Who could even guess what connections she had made, what unspoken loyalties might be brewing behind her silence?

All of them were bound by loyalty, friendship, love. All of them would be useless on a mission.

Worse than useless. Dangerous.

"Kata, are you hearing us?" Ichiro insisted. "You must stay alive."

The drunken man dozing against the wall jerked his

head up, blinked, got to his feet, and wove to the tavern's door. Shortly afterward we could hear a sound like a mighty waterfall thundering into the ditch outside.

"I can't stay alive forever," I said slowly, bringing my thoughts back to the conversation and the cooling bowl of soup in my hands. I swallowed half of its contents and set it down. "No. No, I can't run. I have to get it back."

"Get what back?" Otani eyed me quizzically.

"What she stole from me."

"Who stole what from you, girl?"

"The Takedas' newest daughter-in-law. And what she stole is—my own business." I met the bandit's gaze evenly.

Okiko had betrayed me. So had Jinnai. However, the two of them had only done so because I'd betrayed my own training.

I should never have sent black feathers to my old friends. I should never have asked for their help. And now the only question was how to get away from them and finish my mission alone.

Ichiro was shaking his head. "She won't give it up easily, Kata."

"I won't give her a choice."

"Well, it's all fascinating." Otani drained his wine cup and set it down hard on the table. "But as far as I can see, most of our problems would be solved by getting out of this city. It would certainly be healthier for me to be out-side the walls, and it seems, Flower, that the same is true for you."

I shook my head.

"Girl, as far as I can tell, you've made an enemy of the entire Takeda clan tonight," Otani told me. "And while I do admire your efficiency—"

His words cut off midsentence.

A tall, heavyset man in a short kimono of red-brown silk had opened the wineshop's door. He had a samurai's mustache and topknot and menacing scowl, and he was talking over his shoulder to Shiburo in the entranceway.

"Nonsense. No other wineshops are open, and I'm parched. Don't tell me to stay outside, you sniveling worm, you—" He broke off when his gaze landed on Otani, who was rising to his feet.

"Thief!" he bellowed, drawing the shorter of the two swords by his side. "Where's my horse? My coins? My armor? I'll take your head in exchange!"

As Otani stepped forward a few paces, the angry samurai charged.

The room was small enough that a charge was not the best maneuver. Otani simply stepped sideways to let his opponent crash into a wall, and had his own blade out by the time the enraged man swung around.

The samurai, however, seemed to have some friends.

There were more men crowding in at the entrance, not as grandly dressed or as well-armed as Otani's enemy. Their kimonos were of dull blue cotton; their weapons were clubs and knives. Had the samurai hired some commoners to help apprehend the bandit who'd robbed him?

When one of these newcomers threw a knife that hummed through the air behind Otani's back and headed straight for my left eye, I had my answer.

No, these men had not been hired to help subdue Otani. They were after me.

I dove to one side. Masako, pulling Ozu with her, rolled to the other. The knife buried itself in the wooden wall beside me, and I paused on one knee to wrench it free before leaping to my feet.

In my other hand I snagged an empty bowl and flung it hard into the face of the man who'd thrown the knife. His knees buckled as it hit, which left me free to duck away from a club, pivot, kick, and crack the wrist that held it.

Otani was trading blows with the samurai, who was half a handspan taller and thick in the shoulders as well. Clearly the extra space was taken up with muscle, not brain; the ronin was coolly parrying every furious stroke. But for the moment, his attention was fully occupied.

Yuki ducked a blow from a club and turned to seize her attacker's arm, flinging him over her shoulder and onto our table, shattering it into pieces. Masako shoved Ozu behind her and snatched up a cushion from the floor, flinging it into the face of yet another advancing man. The cushion didn't hurt him, but it did blind him long enough for Ichiro's staff to sweep his feet out from under him.

Now more of these armed commoners were crowding in at the door, pushing back the three dice players, who were struggling to get out. I ducked another club, jabbed my elbow into its owner's stomach as I straightened up, caught a clenched fist and yanked the man attached to it off balance. Unfortunately, I also shoved him into Ichiro, who took a step forward at just the wrong moment. The novice monk fell on top of my attacker, and I had to leap aside from the tangle of their limbs.

This was no place for a fight. It was too close, too cramped, too crowded. I was as likely to get brained from Ichiro's staff as from one of my enemies' cudgels.

The samurai shoved Otani back and lunged after him, bellowing like an enraged bull. Hadn't the fool learned not to charge? He knocked over two of the dice players, who'd retreated from the door. Then he tripped over one of the prone men's legs. Otani raised his sword, ready to finish the man off, but staggered as someone landed a kick on one knee, and his blow missed the target.

Between struggling bodies I caught a glimpse of a familiar figure by the door—the drunk who had gone outside a few minutes ago. I should have seen him as a threat earlier, when he staggered out on first hearing my name. I would have noticed if I hadn't been distracted by a tableful of friends and their concern and their plans and their burdensome presence in the middle of my mission.

Now the man stood steadily and walked soberly. And from behind him stepped a tall, elegant figure in black silk, unmoved by the chaos around. He lowered his head in a quick but courteous bow as his eyes met mine.

Master Ishikawa.

I stamped on the largest remaining piece of the table near my feet, flipped it up, and grabbed it in my left hand, using it to parry a knife that came at me. I swung the chunk of wood at its owner's face and spun to slash with my own knife at an enemy who'd tried to grab me from behind.

Too many. There were too many. One would get in a lucky blow soon, and there was little I could do to prevent it. The only way to win this fight was not to be in it.

I swung the table piece as hard as I could at two men less than a foot away, knocking one into the other so that they both fell sprawling. I could not reach the front door, but there was a window at my back, and on the other side of that window was a river.

I whirled, dropping the chunk of splintered wood from my hand. Here was my chance to leave my friends behind, and it would probably be for their own good as well. I'd have to hope that Master Ishikawa's employees would follow me.

However, the window was blocked. A lithe figure gripped the top of the frame and swung in to land, perfectly balanced, on his feet.

For half a second Jinnai and I were face-to-face, both equally astonished.

Then an arm went around my neck and I was hauled off my feet.

I did not try to get my feet back down; instead, I used the momentum my attacker had given me to swing my knees up, ready to kick Jinnai back through the window and into the river, while at the same time I brought the knife in my hand sharply down, past my hip, and into something soft. The man holding me screamed and the arm around my throat slackened, but my kick went awry and missed the thief as my attacker and I both fell heavily to the floor.

I rolled free and hit the knees of the samurai, who was on his feet once more, attempting to bat aside Otani's sword. The warrior fell on top of me, and I thought my ribs would crack with his weight. Otani heaved the man up and went down himself to a club, which had been aimed for the back of his head but connected with his shoulder blade. On my hands and knees, trying hard to suck air into my lungs, I felt a heavy hand seize hold of my hair just next to the scalp.

"Is she a thief like you?" the samurai roared, and shook me like a dog would shake a rat.

The next moment, a wine cup, thrown by Ozu with all the strength in her wiry little body, cracked him on the bridge of his nose, and he dropped my hair to clutch at the red waterfall pouring down his face and drenching his mustache. I stood upright, my ribs aching, my head spinning, to stare at Jinnai once more.

He was still in front of the broken window, as if too astounded to move. He held something small in one upraised hand.

Something small and round, white and gold.

The pearl.

FOURTEEN

As I struggled to draw in a full breath, as the room wobbled in and out of focus, as crashes and thumps and clangs and yells of warning and cries of pain spun in an eddy around my ears, that tiny bright sphere in Jinnai's hand seemed to center all of my senses.

The pearl.

There's always more to steal, he'd told me. But I hadn't understood. He hadn't meant that the pearl could be easily replaced. He'd meant that he could steal it back from Saiko.

I could save us all now. I could wish. If only I were holding the pearl.

Jinnai could throw it to me, but it was too risky. I might miss it. Someone else might grab it. It could be lost, rolling away under trampling feet, disappearing into a crack between floorboards, gone forever, until the day I died. And then an innocent hand would pick it up and an innocent heart would make a wish.

As long as the pearl was in Jinnai's hand, I could not call

on the services of the demon inside it. But he could—if I gave the pearl to him now.

Should I do that?

Could I trust him?

He'd been my partner. My pursuer. My betrayer—except that he had not betrayed me after all.

Did that mean I'd been wrong about him since the day I dragged him out of a bush in the forest? That he hadn't been following me to steal my treasure for himself?

That he hadn't been lying when he said he'd never lied to me?

I was in the middle of a battle. In the next second, I'd be seized—beaten—maybe killed. I had no time to sort through feelings, identify misjudgments, recalibrate my sense of trust. My spinning brain calculated the odds facing me and seized hold of two simple facts.

One, Jinnai was a thief.

Two, it was better for a thief to have the pearl than to risk it falling back into the hands of Kashihara Saiko.

"It's yours now!" I shouted to Jinnai above the din. "I give it to you! Wish that we're all safe! Do it now!"

Before I could think fully about the fact that I'd just asked Jinnai to risk his soul, another pair of hands closed around my throat and I was dragged backward, feet scrabbling across the floor. My knife made a wild slash through the air. Ichiro, leaping forward to help me, was forced to dodge back to avoid being gutted. The need to breathe rose up in me, crested like a giant wave, and crashed down. I had to breathe—right now, this second. I would kill anyone in this room for one simple, clear, clean gulp of air—

Then the pressure around my throat vanished, and I hit the floor. Sitting there, heaving in sweet breaths, I stared around the wineshop.

The samurai was gone. Master Ishikawa's men were gone, and the master thief as well. There was no sign of Shiburo—had he been wished away by the pearl as well, or had he simply and wisely taken to his heels? The three dice players did remain, but not for long; they crashed through the door in panic and were gone.

Otani got to his knees, rubbing his shoulder, and gazed about him in wonder. Masako wiped blood from her nose as she knelt to assure herself that Ozu was unharmed. Yuki dropped the club she'd been holding and used both hands to smooth her hair back from her face. Ichiro, still holding his staff, swung to the window to face Jinnai.

I sprang up to peer at Jinnai's hand as well, trying to see the pearl more clearly. Was the demon free? Had it taken Jinnai's soul as its payment?

Jinnai's hand was shaking, but I could see both white and gold between his fingers. Then the demon was still imprisoned, which meant we were not in danger of being devoured this moment.

My gaze went to Jinnai's face.

Not that long ago, I'd looked into the face of a man whose soul had been eaten by a demon, glimpsed that foreign and hungry thing staring out of his eyes. Jinnai's eyes did not look like that. They were full of astonishment, horror, fear—and humanity.

Jinnai shuddered. He held the pearl loosely, as if he didn't want to grasp it firmly but didn't dare drop it or fling it aside.

I knew what he was feeling, that rush of harsh cold, as if his heart were pumping tiny needles of ice through his veins. Could he hear the demon laugh? Did he know its delight at being one step closer to freedom?

"What is this?" Jinnai whispered hoarsely. He set wide eyes on me. "What does it do?"

"It's dangerous," I said, taking a step closer to him.

"It's powerful." Jinnai dropped his gaze to the pearl in his unsteady hand. "It's—magic? It grants wishes?"

"At a cost," I said, keeping my voice low, taking another step. I wanted his attention on me, his gaze nowhere else. "Too high a cost. Whatever you do, don't make another wish."

When I'd first handled the pearl, the ring of gold around it had been the width of my thumb. Now it was no thicker than the stem of a slender leaf.

The cut over Jinnai's eyebrow, where I'd hit him earlier, had reopened, and a line of blood was snaking down the side of his face. Slowly, taking care not to startle him, I reached out to touch the red trickle with my fingers.

Then I lowered my hand to his. My bloody fingers brushed the pearl.

"Give it back to me," I told him, my voice so low only the two of us could hear it. I could feel Ichiro's presence close behind me; of all the other people in this room, only he truly knew what was at stake.

Could I count on him to help, if things went wrong? If Jinnai refused to give me the pearl—if he tried to make a second wish—would Ichiro help me kill him?

If the two of us were wise, we'd kill the young thief

now, before he understood just what he held. The thought filled me with revulsion. I hadn't wanted to kill Jinnai two days earlier, when I'd tied him to a tree. I didn't want to do so now.

But if he were mad and reckless enough to try for another wish, I might have to.

If he were mad and reckless enough to try for another wish, I might not be able to.

And he was that mad, wasn't he? He was certainly mad and reckless enough to claim that he loved me.

"It'll take your soul," I warned Jinnai. It seemed as if I should be able to feel the power of the pearl between our two hands, as if the thing should burn like a living coal. But it only felt cool and smooth and hard, smeared with both our blood. "Give it back to me, Jinnai. Say the words," I whispered. "Please."

Jinnai smiled.

As if it were a matter of no great importance, he pulled his hand away and let the pearl drop into my palm. It was so small, so light, I had to look at it to be sure it was there.

"It's yours," Jinnai said easily. "I stole it back for you. I always meant to. I told you, there's nothing I can't steal."

I could not tell if the shudder that swept from my scalp all the way down my back was shock, or relief, or fear.

Jinnai seemed about to laugh. I didn't know what expression, beyond surprise, was on my face, but apparently he found it amusing.

"Kata," Ichiro said from behind me, a warning in his voice. "I think we should leave."

I turned to look at him, and he nodded at the window behind Jinnai.

Jinnai turned to look as well. He gave a strangled yelp and, in a complicated movement, twitched sideways and jumped backward at the same time.

On every square of rice paper, even those that hung torn and tattered in their frames, an eye had appeared, as if drawn with ink by the most skillful hand and with the finest brush. But these eyes were made of more than ink. They blinked and opened wide to study us. Each iris and pupil turned and shifted, tracking our every movement.

Ozu choked back a frightened squeak and plastered herself against Masako's side.

"Moku-moku ren," Ichiro said quietly. "They won't hurt us, but they might be a sign. Other things could be stirring now that a wish has been made."

"Other things?" Otani asked from across the room. "What other things, exactly? I'd like to know what I'm fighting."

"You're not fighting anything," I said as I pocketed the pearl. I turned on my heel and made for the door of the wineshop, reaching out a hand to slide it open.

It was time to do what I'd decided. Time to complete my mission alone.

But my hand jerked back when I saw that the door's screen, too, was covered with curious eyes, watching me eagerly, as if impatient to know what I would do next.

"Don't be absurd, Kata. You're not going anywhere by yourself." Masako was at my side, Ozu clinging to her hand.

Ichiro moved quickly as well. "I laid this burden on you, Kata. Do you think I'd abandon you now?"

Jinnai, too, stepped forward. "Haven't I shown you how difficult I am to leave behind?"

Yuki only shook her head.

Otani, having sheathed his sword, stood silent, his arms crossed over his chest, frowning as if he were thinking hard. He didn't seem to have anything to add.

"No," I said shortly. I reached for the screen again, and every eye upon it swiveled to watch my hand.

Once I got outside, I could take to the rooftops. Even Jinnai would not be able to keep up with me. All I had to do was slide the door open.

If only it weren't *looking* at me like that.

Ichiro edged past me. He put his hands together and bowed to the eyes on the screen. "Pardon us. We have to get by," he said, and the eyes turned to him and blinked and watched as he slid the screen gingerly open and stepped through.

"Bow," he told us from the entranceway beyond. "They're mostly harmless, but—"

"Mostly?" Otani inquired.

"It doesn't hurt to be polite," Ichiro said simply. "Even to bakemono."

Especially, I thought, and bowed humbly to the eyes on the screen as I slipped past. Behind me, Otani edged sideways through the doorway, determined not to touch the frame. The others, equally cautious, came after him.

Once safely out of the door, we crossed the narrow

plank bridge over the ditch that ran alongside the wine-shop. Something hissed and splashed in the murky water below, barely visible in the light from a single paper lantern hanging from the side of the building.

My eyes were on the rooftops, scanning them for the easiest way up, when Ichiro spoke. "Things are stirring already," he said grimly.

"Yes. They are."

The new voice seemed to arrive out of the air, and its owner with it. Where had she come from? Out of an alley? From behind a fence? In that filthy little street, her snow-white kimono was spotless. An ornament as delicate as frozen leaves shimmered in her silky hair.

Otani's sword rose, but I shook my head to keep him from attacking. The woman who was now standing beside me merely smiled. The smile was the only thing about her that wasn't lovely. It was too wide, had too many teeth. And somehow it always looked . . . hungry.

"You'll need to hurry," she said, speaking only to me, without even a glance for the others. Her voice was low and slightly rough, and it made me think of deep burrows, warm fur, something brown and soft and rich. "Your instincts were correct before. Get it off the island. It's too powerful now, too close to freedom. It will call to every bakemono it can awaken and try to use them. If they can force you to make one last wish, the demon in the pearl will be released."

I nodded.

"I cannot help you much once you leave the shore,

but there may be others who can," she said. And then she changed. A storm of fur and silk, skin and hide, swirled in the darkness, and a white fox darted down the street, away into the night.

"Ah." Jinnai shook his head, as though he were trying to rattle his brains into better working order. "Did that just—did she actually—did I really see . . .?"

"A woman turn into a fox? I'm relieved to hear I'm not the only one doubting my own eyes." Otani looked from Jinnai, to the street where the fox spirit had disappeared, to me. "Well, Flower, I always did have the feeling that you were on a mission you told no one about. I didn't know it was for the gods."

Ichiro was nodding. "It makes sense, what she said, Kata. All demons have their territories, the places where they are the most powerful. But the demon in the pearl—I think its territory may be this entire island. Out at sea, its power should die down. We have to get you safely to the harbor."

"We?" Otani lifted an eyebrow.

I shook my head. "Not all of you." I turned to face Masako.

I didn't quite know how I would get rid of my followers, but at least I could make sure that my oldest friend would not be a part of what we were about to face. "Get her to safety," I said, pointing to Ozu. Masako opened her mouth to protest. "Don't argue," I growled.

Masako didn't. She merely reached out to embrace me, her cheek wet and cool against mine.

We had no time for farewells, no time for tears, but my

hands tightened on her arms until I could feel the strength of the bones beneath her smooth muscles.

"This debt can never be repaid," she said softly, in my ear. Then she let me go, seized Ozu's hand, and pulled her away, running down the street, rounding a curve of the river, lost to the night in moments. Trust a girl trained by Madame Chiyome to understand what needed to be done and to waste no words where words could do no good.

Two gone. I turned to the rest.

"Don't argue," Ichiro said. "We're taking you to the harbor."

Jinnai nodded. Yuki simply looked stubborn. And how could I argue with a girl who would not argue?

Otani, though—he was another matter.

"This isn't your fight," I told the bandit, before the other three could interfere. "This is—something different. Unnatural."

"You'd leave me out, would you?" he said, with an expression I could not read.

"You're a warrior," I told him. "But this is not what you've been trained for. The things out there—you won't know how to fight them. But they can still kill you."

"I died a long time ago," he said, and before I could begin to understand what he meant by that, he smiled. "Still, this sounds like the kind of fight I wouldn't want to miss. Oh, don't bother, Flower. As far as I can tell, you don't have time to waste arguing with us."

I closed my mouth and set my teeth. He was right. If they wouldn't leave willingly, I couldn't fight them *and* every demon between here and the ocean.

That didn't mean I couldn't escape, however. For the moment, though, it was best to let them think they'd won.

"Then you do as I say," I told all four. "At every turn."

"Your loyal retainers, Commander Flower," Otani said, his shorter sword already in his hand, his gaze moving purposefully up and down the street. It was empty now; even the latest revelers were snoring on their mats or in alleys, or perhaps frightened away by the chaos that had overtaken Shiburo's wineshop.

"To the harbor, then?" Jinnai asked. "Follow me."

Jinnai did not take us through streets or alleys, but set a quick pace along the riverbank. We crossed behind wineshops and warehouses and rows of cramped and shabby houses, climbed over heaps of trash, picked our way through gardens, and stepped carefully past encampments of sleepers huddled on the bare ground. Whenever someone woke to curse at us, Jinnai always knew his name and would call out a quick reassuring word that made the sleeper's head sink down once more.

My back prickled and the skin along my neck tingled, alert to the danger in the darkness all around us. I caught Ichiro's eye and knew he was thinking what I was.

Yuki had seen only a little of what the pearl could awaken. The other two, Otani and Jinnai, had probably heard fireside tales of ghosts and demons, but never met so much as a tengu flitting through a forest or a kappa lurking in a stream, disguised as a smooth, round stone.

They did not know, as Ichiro and I did, what it was to

come face-to-face with bakemono.

There had been a time when I'd easily assumed that the world of bakemono could never be the world I lived in day to day. Back then, I'd believed that only a trick of the light could make a shadow, glimpsed from the corner of my eye, seem to pounce on its prey. I'd thought only moles or rats scuttled in the bushes at night, that a despairing cry echoing in the darkness could only be an owl's call.

That was before I'd fought tiny scuttling creatures swollen to the size of monsters, shadows that grew teeth and claws, scraps of mist that could grip like iron fetters. Before I'd encountered a pitiful, half-drowned child who wanted to drag me into the depths beside her, a generous hostess whose smiles and hair hid her true nature—and her true hunger.

A cat with two tails. A fox who could turn into a woman.

Bakemono were everywhere.

And at least three members of my inconvenient little army would have slim idea how to deal with them.

When we reached a bridge, Jinnai took us over the river, and we plunged into the pleasure district. Even here, most stores and wineshops and theaters were closed, and only a few windows still glowed. As we passed those lighted screens, flickers spread across the rice paper, and more painted eyes opened to watch us.

Jinnai ducked around a corner into a narrow alley between two silent buildings. The eaves of both roofs nearly met overhead, blocking out most of the moonlight.

Abruptly the thief came to a stop.

"What? Are you lost?" Otani called out impatiently from behind me.

"No!" Jinnai announced indignantly. "Someone built a wall."

Otani snorted. "He's lost. Back the way we came."

"I'm not lost. I'm never lost," Jinnai was insisting when the darkness around us suddenly grew denser. Something had cut off the faint light remaining from the few glowing windows in the street behind us.

Yuki moved closer to me. Ichiro drew in his breath.

There came a stifled grunt from the mouth of the alley, as though Otani had walked into something. A moment later, he came blundering back.

"Someone . . . well, someone built a wall there, too," he said, bewildered.

Something ran over my foot.

I stepped back, kicking the thing off. It flew through the air and hit the ground with a startled squeak. A rat.

"Nurikabe." Ichiro's voice came out of the darkness.

"What's that?" I asked impatiently. Something was tickling at the edge of my hearing. It wasn't quite a sound yet, but it would be so momentarily. If the others would stop talking, I might be able to figure out what it was.

Yuki put her shoulder against mine. I could feel her listening, just as I was doing.

"Does it matter? We're trapped." I heard the whisper of oiled metal on leather as one of Otani's swords slid from its sheath.

"A living wall. And we're not trapped." That was Ichiro's voice.

"Put that away. You'll skewer one of us," Jinnai told Otani.

"I think I know how to handle a sword, little thief who led us into a blind alley."

"Just let me—" Ichiro's voice cut off as he walked into something. The wall? Jinnai?

"Watch yourself, monk!"

Clearly, what Ichiro had walked into was Otani.

"I know what to—"

"Quiet, all of you!" My voice rang out in frustration, startling the three of them, cutting their bickering short.

But not everything was silent.

That sound teasing at my ears had gotten louder. A soft scuttling, a scratching. A sound of claws gripping, of furry bellies and naked tails brushing against dry straw.

"Look up," Ichiro said sharply.

On the closest roof, outlined against a dim gray glow of moonlight and starlight, something was sitting. The little upright shape was about the size of a lapdog, but the head was too small, and the ears were as well. It looked like a rat, though larger than any such creature should be. I caught a glimpse of viciously curved teeth that did not gleam white or ivory in the moonlight. They shone as bright as a polished sword.

Then the rats were upon us.

FIFTEEN

The rats were on my feet, climbing toward my knees, claws pricking. None of their teeth had bit, not yet, but the creatures squealed and chattered, sounding hungry.

Jinnai yelped. Otani cursed. I heard the ronin's sword clang against the ground, but even if he managed to slice one rat in two, there were a hundred more.

The large, steel-toothed rat on the rooftop hissed eagerly.

"Don't fall!" Ichiro shouted. "Whatever you do, don't fall over! And let me get closer to that wall!"

He must have pushed Jinnai aside, for the thief thumped into me. I stumbled backward, away from Yuki, and stepped on something warm and wriggling. Staggering, I lost my balance. To my relief, my shoulder blades hit a wooden wall behind me. It kept me upright, but it couldn't protect me from the furry waterfall that poured over my head from the roof above.

Trapped. Trapped between walls that should not have been here, trapped by tiny creatures that should be no threat at all. Claws ripped at my hair. A soft weight pressed on my eyes. Bare tails lashed at my neck. I grabbed handfuls of fur and snatched rats from my face and head, flinging them away.

But there were more, there were always more. They'd pile into this small space, and we'd be helpless. Someone would fall, soon. Someone would trip, or the weight of a hundred, a thousand, little bodies would pull one of us down.

The thought of being crushed, buried, smothered in warm fur, clawed and nibbled to death, was worse than any idea of dying in an honest fight. I leaped up, grabbing the rooftop above me, seizing handfuls of prickly thatch. Keeping my eyes and mouth tightly closed, ignoring the rats that poured over my head and shoulders, I thrashed and kicked. Someone beneath me grabbed one of my feet and shoved, giving me the height I needed.

Then I was crouched on the roof, face-to-face with the steel-toothed rat.

The smaller rats scuttled away, as if to give their master space. It bared its shining teeth at me in a feral grin, and I bared mine back.

I could see the muscles in its back legs bunching as it tensed, its tail writhing like a worm in the straw. So I tensed my legs as well, and when the rat leaped, I rolled away and came up running.

The huge rat squealed as its leap took it over the edge

of the roof. I didn't know how it would fare in the alley among my friends. I didn't know how my friends would fare, facing that creature. But I was running at last, leaving them all behind.

Smaller rats fled as I vaulted over the roof's peak, let the downward slope increase my speed, and hurdled the gap between this building and the next.

Shouts and squeals faded behind me. I ran from rooftop to rooftop, the moon lighting my way. My friends would have to fight off the steel-toothed rat and its furry army, but that would be the last fight they'd have to face for my sake.

From now on, I'd rely on no one but myself. Risk no one but myself.

With only the demon in my pocket for company, I headed toward the sea. My feet were so light over tile and thatch, I felt as if, any moment, I would leap and fail to come down. I'd fly.

It was one of the city's temples, eventually, that brought me to earth. I managed to get from a wineshop to a tree to the wall that surrounded the sacred grounds; from there it was just a leap to the kitchen and storehouse, then to the hall where the monks ate their meals, and then to the bell tower. There, at last, I was stranded.

Below me stretched a garden, pale paths winding among boulders and around smooth pools. Beyond the garden was a stand of cedars and pines with a towering camphor tree in the center, all the branches melding together to make a clot of pure black on the nighttime landscape. Past them I could glimpse, once more, the temple wall.

I could backtrack and make my way along that wall, but it would probably be faster to go straight ahead. That would avoid the risk of Jinnai or any of the others catching up with me.

Slipping off the tower's tiled roof, I landed as lightly as I could on a thick bed of moss. I left footprints behind, but at least I made little noise.

Ignoring the paths, which curved and wound gracefully to encourage strolling monks in their meditation, I headed straight for the trees, feeling a tremor of relief when their shadow fell across my shoulders. Darkness had always been my ally. I'd be safe within it from restless monks who could not sleep, from friends who might try to follow me.

There was a trail under my bare feet; I could feel its smoothness. I headed quickly along it, one arm up in front of my face to guard against spiky branches.

I breathed in the tang of cedar and pine, the cool, damp air that never, even in full daylight, was free of shadow. The trail took me ahead, deeper into the trees, deeper into darkness.

It couldn't be large, this strand of trees. Any moment I'd duck under the last branch. I'd see the wall before me, stones glimmering in the moonlight. I'd climb it and be back on the streets, heading down toward the sea.

It would be easy. I didn't need Jinnai to guide me through this city. I didn't need anybody.

The path seemed to be narrowing. I could feel branches brushing my shoulders, the sweep of pine needles, the prickle of cedar. I shuffled forward, feet close together, so I wouldn't step off the path and lose it. I might never find it again in this darkness.

This darkness.

Somehow, the shadows around me didn't feel cool and friendly anymore. My own breath felt hot and sticky against my face. And the night itself seemed to be closing in. It took all my strength to push through it.

Where was that wall? Where was the moonlight, the free air, the streets where I could run? How could this wood be so large, here in the heart of the Takedas' largest city?

I inched forward. Was the path curving? What if it turned and took me back to the garden?

I was moving so slowly. Too slowly. But if I tried to run, or even walk more quickly, I'd lose the path.

A root snagged my foot, and I stumbled, biting back a hiss of pain and stepping into a drift of dried pine needles, soft and slithering beneath my feet. Quickly I righted myself, my toes groping for bare, smooth earth.

I couldn't find it.

I backed up a cautious half-step and swept the ground with my feet to either side. Nothing but more needles, shifting under my weight.

I dropped to my knees, reaching out with my hands. Dry needles. Roots like frozen snakes. Fallen branches sticky with sap.

The path was gone.

I wasted minutes hunting frantically for it, and at last gave up. I raised both arms to shield my face and began walking blindly forward, thrusting my shoulders against branches and needles, tripping over roots and deadwood, struggling against the darkness. It didn't even matter now what direction I went. If I kept going straight, I'd force a way through.

My breath began to quicken, hot in my mouth, tasting of pine sap and something more sour. Of disappointment. Frustration.

Failure.

I should have been free of this wood by now. I should have been up on the temple wall, high enough to see any threat coming at me. I should be running through the sleeping city.

I shouldn't be stumbling through this endless wood, smothering in greenery. When would I get out?

Maybe I never would.

Maybe I didn't deserve to.

I wouldn't be able to get down to the harbor. Not in time. I'd fail. I should have expected it. I'd failed so many times.

If I'd simply done what I was supposed to do, what I'd been trained to do, on my very first mission, I wouldn't be here now. I'd thought I was so good—the best—and look where I'd ended up.

Lost in a forest. Defeated by trees.

I shoved my way forward, my breath catching with frustration. Masako had cried like this, I remembered. When I'd cracked her wrist in the practice yard, rehearsing a maneuver we'd been taught earlier that day. She'd always been slow to catch on to a new move; I'd always been quick. That time, she hadn't had her balance right, hadn't been able to resist me, and I'd twisted too hard and left her sobbing in the dirt.

She got an extra blow with the bamboo rod for letting her pain show.

How old had we been? Ten? Twelve?

We should have been friends. I think we were, for a while. We laid our mats out side by side, our sore and aching muscles eased by each other's warmth.

But I was defter than she was with every weapon. Faster in every race. I could hold my breath longer underwater, climb a rope more easily, go longer without food.

Friendship is a weakness. You have enemies and you have rivals. Nothing more.

One night I moved my mat away from Masako's. From then on I slept alone.

She sobbed that night, too.

Friendship is a weakness.

They taught us all that, but I was the only one who believed it.

Most of the other girls found some way to keep a secret kernel of tenderness in their hearts. Masako mothered the younger girls. Yuki tended her plants. Aki and Okiko clung to each other.

Okiko had turned on me, though. And she'd been right to do it. I should never have asked my old friends to help me safeguard the pearl.

Look what had happened to them. Aki struck down by her own sister. Masako in tears as she fled with Ozu. Yuki and Ichiro, Otani and Jinnai, probably dead by now, trapped helplessly, devoured by filthy vermin.

Jinnai . . .

Jinnai had stolen the pearl back from Saiko for me, and how had I rewarded him? By asking him to risk his soul.

I should never have become the pearl's guardian. I was doomed to fail, and to drag anyone who tried to help down with me.

It would be best if I simply stopped trying.

I'd already given up pushing against the entangling branches. I leaned my weight against them and drew in a slow breath.

How odd. My knife was in my hand, and I couldn't remember drawing it.

I stroked the flat of the blade gently across my palm. It wasn't my own—a shadow warrior's weapon. If it had been, the blade would have been black with grease and soot, so it would not catch the light. This was just a poor man's knife, with a worn wooden handle. The edge was not even that sharp.

Sharp enough. It broke through the skin of my palm, and I barely felt the pain.

Just one flick of the tip in the right spot, and it would all be over. I could sit down here, alone in the center of this suffocating forest, and let my life slowly ebb like the tide leaving the shore.

I could stop struggling. Stop fighting.

I could fail. It was astonishing how restful that thought was.

Yet something held me back. Some faint memory of an obligation.

Oh, yes. What about the pearl?

I had no will left to care about my burden. It wasn't mine by rights, anyway. Ichiro had only given it to me because he'd been in fear for his own life.

And I'd been no good as a guardian. I had wished, again and again. Now the demon inside was just a hairsbreadth away from freedom.

It would be for the best if I let the pearl lie here with my body. Someone else would pick it up one day.

Someone like Saiko, probably.

The thought seemed to freeze my hand on the handle of my knife. The blade hesitated against my skin.

Had I truly thought of letting the pearl lie here for Saiko to find?

That wasn't right.

I might be tired. I might be a failure. But I wasn't going to hand the pearl over to *Saiko*.

If that thought had arisen inside my head, then something was wrong with my thoughts.

I gripped the hilt of the knife hard and thrust the blade into the trunk of the nearest tree. I thought the wood quivered under the blow.

I forced myself to my feet.

There was an enemy here. I knew it now. My instincts, awake at last, were screaming at me to fight.

Fight what?

There was no demon to face. Unless . . .

Could this forest itself be the demon? How could I fight a forest?

I turned, reaching out with my hands, but thick

branches hung with dense curtains of needles shut me in on every side. How had I gotten here, if I couldn't even take a step? Had the trees moved to entrap me, imprisoning my body, poisoning my mind?

Light. Light was flashing through the dark needles.

Someone was calling. "Kata!" The trees were pressing on me. I felt as if my ribs would cave in; my lungs were empty of air.

Hands thrust through the greenery and seized mine, and suddenly I could take a step, and then another. Jinnai yanked me forward, and the trees seemed somehow to fall back. I stood face-to-face with the thief in a little clearing. Otani was behind him, with a torch in his hand. Yuki tugged Jinnai aside to get a look at me, and Ichiro, peering over her shoulder, heaved a sigh of relief.

"The forest," I gasped out, my voice uneven as my breath shuddered back into my lungs. "The forest is a demon."

Otani peered at me. "It's hardly a forest, Flower. Just a few cedars."

"We have to get out," I insisted.

"Fine, we'll get out," Jinnai said impatiently. "Then I'll put a leash on you, I swear, Kata, to keep you from running away again. Wait—you're hurt." He let go of my right hand to cup my left in both of his.

"She's right," Ichiro said grimly. "Look there."

He pointed. Every eye followed his gaze.

My knife was buried up to its hilt in the knobby trunk of an old pine. The sticky liquid oozing from the gash and dripping down the rough bark was not sap.

The tree was bleeding.

"The forest *is* a demon," Ichiro said. "And I think Kata made it angry. We have to go."

Jinnai pulled me away from the wounded tree. "Yes. Certainly. We're leaving now!" he called out, raising his voice. "Sorry to intrude, humblest apologies, won't happen again—"

"The path," Otani interrupted. "Where's the path?"

SIXTEEN

All four of my companions turned to look at the unbroken wall of branches and dark green needles that blocked our way on every side.

"It wants to keep us here," I said, my voice still quavering with shameful weakness. "And it tries to—"

Ichiro gave me a sharp look.

How could I admit it? How could I say that this forest had very nearly made me defeat myself?

"It will try to get into your thoughts," Ichiro said. "The longer we stay, the worse it will be. This way."

"How can you tell the way?" Otani demanded.

Ichiro held up a coarse bit of string, unraveled from the hem of his robe. The other end disappeared between two close-set trees.

"I thought we might need a way out," he said. "Follow me."

I wrenched my knife from the tree's trunk, slid it into

the sheath at my wrist, and did as he said.

Ichiro's fragile thread led us stumbling between trees, forcing ourselves through underbrush, crawling over roots, ducking under branches. Yuki stayed close behind the novice monk; Jinnai brought up the rear with me, his grip firm on my bloody hand. Otani walked in the middle. The light of his torch seemed to keep the menacing trees at bay.

"We're lost," he muttered.

"We're not lost," Ichiro called back.

"We were only in this wood a few minutes before we found Kata. We've already been walking for longer than that."

"We're following the thread," Ichiro insisted.

"We're going in circles. We're lost." Otani's steps were slowing. He lowered his torch. "We're lost," he repeated.

Jinnai pushed at his shoulder. "Move. Don't stand there."

Otani did not obey. He stood, looking from side to side as if he'd seen something that had caught his attention and confused him, all at once. "I lost them," he said vaguely.

"Who?" Jinnai shoved at him again, but it was like a mouse shoving a mountain.

"All of them," the ronin answered, turning his head from side to side.

Were the trees drawing in? Darker, denser? Was Otani's torch dimming?

Jinnai let go of my hand.

"They trusted me. They followed me," Otani murmured. "Everyone said it would be glory, but it was only death. Masatoshi, Nakatada, even Aritake . . . all gone now. Can't you hear them?"

The torch slipped from his hand, landing on a bed of damp moss. I snatched it up before it could go out.

"Ichiro!" I shouted, but the muffling closeness of pine and cedar needles seemed to choke all the strength from my voice. "Which way?"

Ichiro turned to me, his face the gray-white of wet ashes. A broken piece of thread dangled from his fingers.

Jinnai stumbled a pace or two away from me. "Stay close," I told him, reaching out to snag his sleeve.

"Where did she go?" he whispered.

"Where did *who* go?" I demanded impatiently. As far as I could tell, we were all here. That was the problem—we *couldn't* leave.

"She's gone. She left. She left me." Jinnai's face crumpled with misery, and he looked six years old instead of seventeen.

"I'm sorry," Otani mumbled, laying a hand on the hilt of his shorter sword, loosening it in the sheath. "I should be dead, too, I should be dead, I should be . . ."

Yuki's face was wet with silent tears.

Jinnai twisted his arm against my grasp. I dug my fingers in. "What did I do wrong?" he muttered, shutting his eyes, shaking his head. "They all like me. Everyone does. Everyone but her." His eyes opened to stare at me. "And you," he whispered.

"Ichiro!" I shouted frantically. "Which way?"

Every time my eyes shifted to a tree close by, I felt as if another, out of my line of sight, shuffled closer still.

"I don't know," Ichiro gasped. "I'm sorry. I don't know. I can't do anything right. My sister could tell. My uncle, too.

Even my father, he knew. How weak I am. How useless. Everyone always knew."

We were trapped. The forest had us, and it was all my fault. My friends had come to find me, and they were going to die for it.

Still clinging to Jinnai, I used my other hand to swing the flickering torch at the encroaching trees. "Get back!" I shouted. "Get away!"

But I didn't know how to fight this kind of demon.

Yuki slid to her knees. "Don't give in," I growled at her.

She held a small black berry, oozing sticky juice, between her fingers. She looked down at it, and then back up at me. She pointed.

"That way?" I asked.

She nodded.

I held the torch high and dragged Jinnai along, shouting at Ichiro to bring Otani, following Yuki as she darted between two trees. Did she truly know which way to go? Or was she only pursuing a phantom that the trees had stirred in her brain? I didn't know. But I knew that movement might save us. Standing still was death.

And Yuki *did* seem to know where she was going. She ducked under a curtain of glossy green leaves that nearly swept the ground. I didn't dare hesitate. Pulling Jinnai behind me, I did the same. Ichiro and Otani shoved their way through a moment later.

We were under a vast dome of branches, free of the prickly closeness of pine and cedar. Here there was space to move and air to breathe.

More of the small black berries that Yuki had found earlier crunched beneath my bare feet. A sharp, stinging smell rose to my nose. Camphor. We were under the canopy of the ancient camphor tree I'd glimpsed from the bell tower.

The crisp scent, something like medicine, seemed to clear my mind a little. Otani and Jinnai stood, blinking in bewilderment, and Ichiro shook his head in wonder.

Yuki laid both hands on the deeply furrowed trunk of the camphor tree. She touched her forehead to it.

"This isn't one of the bakemono trees," Ichiro said reverently. "It has its own spirit."

He put both hands together and bowed respectfully. Then he gave me a pointed look until I did the same.

"It's protecting us?" he asked Yuki.

She looked up and nodded.

"But we can't stay here," I said. We couldn't cling to this tree forever, no matter how kindly it might feel. I still had to reach the harbor.

The forest had nearly defeated us before. Was there any way through it?

Well, there was one. My hand twitched toward my pocket.

The fox had warned me that the demon in the pearl would try to trap me, forcing me to make one last wish.

Had it succeeded? Was I caught between making a wish and setting a demon free—or staying here until we were forced by thirst or hunger out among the demon trees once more, to drown in our own misery?

Yuki blotted her wet face with her sleeve and pointed again.

"You can get us out of here?" Otani asked, his voice ragged. He turned to me. "How does she know?"

I looked at Yuki, saw the certainty on her face. I shrugged.

"She knows," I said.

Yuki didn't even seem to need the sputtering torch I still held as she led us between close-set trunks and clinging branches. She'd always been at home among plants, I thought, as I sweated and stumbled in her wake. Even a forest of bakemono trees could not steal that from her.

The dark thoughts might be crowding in on her, as they were on me. But still, she knew her way.

I hoped.

Otherwise, we were all doomed. And the pearl would lie shining among serpentine roots and heaps of evergreen needles, among my bones, until the day—

No. I recognized those thoughts. I pushed them away.

Now, even with my night vision ruined by the torch I held, I could glimpse a gray shimmer up ahead. Moonlight on stones. Then I was ducking under one last, low branch, pulling Jinnai with me, twisting free of a clawed twig that tried to snatch at my hair, turning in the fresh, cool air to see Otani and Ichiro stagger from the trees as well.

We were out. We were free.

Before us was the temple wall, more than twice my height. Behind us, the forest melted away to a stand of cedars only a few trees thick, with a camphor in the center and a garden on the other side.

Otani rubbed both hands across his face, not so much to clear away tears, I thought, as to hide for a moment. Jinnai shuddered. He dropped my hand. Ichiro drew in a long breath and let it out slowly.

"None of it was true," he said firmly, looking at each of us in turn. "That was a demon turning our own thoughts into weapons."

"Are you so sure, little monk?" Otani let his hands fall, and his face, showing dimly in the torchlight, was bleak. But at least he did not seem inclined to atone for the deaths in his past by drawing his sword against himself.

"Are you giving up the fight so easily?" Ichiro answered, with just the right steel in his tone to make Otani's back stiffen.

"We can't spend time talking," I told them. Thanks and gratitude and even regret would have to wait.

Ichiro nodded. "Kata still has to get to the harbor." And he turned his gaze to the temple wall.

"I'm no spider," Otani objected, looking up as well.

I surveyed my little army. Yuki, Jinnai, and I all knew how to scale a wall. Ichiro might have learned some new skills during his two years in a temple full of warrior monks, but climbing walls was unlikely to be among them. As for Otani, with two swords through his belt and heavy armor under his rough clothes—there was no chance.

"The two of you go around. Not back through the wood," I said quickly, and thrust the torch into Ichiro's hands. "If you meet any monks, Ichiro can talk them into letting you out through the gate. Meet us at the harbor if you can. Yuki, Jinnai—" I nodded at the wall.

"Wait."

Before we could start to climb, Jinnai gently took my bloody hand in both of his. Working swiftly but precisely he used a strip torn from his cloth belt to bind up the cut across my palm.

"Hands are important," he said quietly, glancing up at me as he tied the bandage. "My mother taught me that."

His fingers were warm, and the tight bandage eased the pain I had not been letting myself feel. I looked into his clever, narrow face, ruddy in the torchlight, and felt words shrivel on my tongue.

What did I owe him—all of them? Thanks? Apologies? Promises? Warnings?

I didn't know. All I could do was nod my gratitude to Jinnai. He smiled.

"Here, Flower," Otani said, dropping to one knee and cupping his hands. I stepped into the support he'd made, and he lifted me to his shoulders. From there I easily found cracks for my toes and fingers. It was not long before I was at the top of the wall.

Otani gave the same help to Yuki and Jinnai, and they followed. As they climbed, I glanced down at Ichiro and Otani, the monk and the bandit, in their pool of torchlight below us.

We couldn't risk noise. I lifted a hand in farewell. Ichiro smiled back. Otani gave me a mock bow.

One by one, Jinnai, Yuki, and I dropped down onto the streets of the dark and sleeping town.

"No more alleys," I told Jinnai. He nodded and dashed along a lane of shuttered shops. Yuki and I came after him. We turned quickly left, then right, and arrived at the wide avenue that led downhill from Ryujin's shrine to the harbor.

The air was fresher here, and the night was beginning to fade. Blue tinged the gray along the horizon. Jinnai was running easily alongside me, Yuki at my back, and now we could see the boats, dark dreaming shapes in the water, bristling with masts that stood straight and black against the slowly lightening sky.

Thin threads of smoke were spiraling up from the small huts near the shore, and a few fishermen were emerging, heading for their boats. They were on their way to catch the retreating tide—and I needed to do the same.

The huge ship I'd had my eye on earlier was still at the jetty. Two square sails had been hoisted, ready to fill with wind and move the vessel away from the shore. Only the anchor rope at the stern and the lines tied to the jetty were holding it in place.

I began to spit curses in short bursts between my teeth each time one of my feet hit the ground. We'd be too late. Once the ship pulled away from the jetty, how could I sneak on board?

"They're still loading cargo," Jinnai puffed at my side. "There, look!" Two bearers were jogging up the jetty, carrying a bundle slung from a pole balanced on their shoulders. A man standing near the ship—I took him to be in command, from his wide-legged, confident stance and his exasperated shouts—waved at them to hurry.

We did the opposite, slowing down as we approached the harbor. No need to catch all eyes with our frantic pace. By the time we reached the stony beach, we were walking sedately, even as impatience and frustration burned in my gut and heart.

We ducked beneath the jetty, and my hand flicked my knife out. A figure was sitting slumped on the wet, muddy stones, her back against one of the pilings. She lifted her head. Blood was smeared across one cheek. Dull eyes tracked our approach, and I felt a snarl rise in my throat.

Okiko? Here?

But in the next moment I realized I'd been wrong. This was not the traitor who'd sold me to Saiko.

This was her sister.

SEVENTEEN

Yuki threw herself down by Aki's side. Her quick, deft hands tugged the girl upright, patting at her shoulders, her ribs, her stomach. A faint cry escaped Aki's lips when Yuki pressed too hard.

Yuki's eyes met mine. She held up bloody fingers.

"I'm sorry, Kata," Aki mumbled, her words slurred. "I couldn't kill her."

I came to kneel beside her.

"She betrayed the mission," Aki whispered. "She betrayed . . ." Her voice trailed off, as if she were waiting for someone else to finish her sentence.

"You. Me. Everything," she said weakly, when no one did.

I knew that even if Yuki could stitch up Aki's wound, stop the bleeding, keep infection at bay, she would never be whole again.

I'm the one who is sorry, I wanted to tell her. *I should never have sent you the black feather. I should never have called on your help.*

But I had no time. The tide was slowly but steadily pulling away from the land.

I turned to Yuki instead. "Stay with her. Take care of her."

Yuki nodded. And then, her voice husky and raw as if every word hurt, barely audible over the low growl of the surf against the shore, she said the only thing that could have saved Aki.

"We are all your sisters now," she told her.

I got back up, sheathing my knife, to take hold of Jinnai's sleeve and pull him away. Yuki also rose, lifting Aki to her feet. She helped the injured girl up the beach.

I should have left the twins to their acrobatics, Yuki to her herbs and potions, Masako to her family. I should never have drawn them into a mission that was none of theirs.

These were not thoughts whispered to me by some demonic forest hungry for my life. These were simple truths.

If I'd left my friends alone, Aki and Okiko would still be sisters. Otani would not have been within a breath of drawing his sword against himself. And Jinnai would not have risked his soul.

My heart contracted inside my chest, withered to powdery dust, and fell apart, leaving me hollow, empty, alone.

Except, of course, for Jinnai.

"What next?" he asked, watching soberly as Yuki helped the limping Aki away.

I wished I knew. If I'd had more time to study the ship

earlier, I might have a plan. As it was, I just had a single, faint hope—a hope that might serve Jinnai as well as myself by getting him far away from me.

"Can you create a diversion?" I asked the thief.

"What kind?"

"Anything. Steal something from the cargo. Push the captain off the jetty. It doesn't matter, as long as they're not watching what I do."

Jinnai nodded. He took a step or two into the ocean, eyeing the jetty overhead. He seemed ready to jump up and swing himself onto the boards, but a stone turned underfoot and he fell into the water with a startled squawk.

The stone Jinnai had slipped on, green with moss and slime, rolled into deeper water as if he'd kicked it loose while falling. Then it bobbed to the surface.

A stone? Floating?

As Jinnai sat up, soaked and shivering, the stone sprouted clawed arms, spindly legs, and a head like a turtle's—except I'd never seen a turtle with malignant eyes and a mouthful of spiky teeth.

Jinnai saw the kappa at the same moment I did, and floundered away with a look of horror and a great deal of splashing. I leaped, grabbing hold of a beam overhead, the holes and hollows in the ancient wood giving my fingers purchase. Then I swung my feet to kick the vile little creature out to sea where the current seized it and swirled it away, just as startled heads appeared over the edge of the jetty to stare at Jinnai.

I don't know what Jinnai might have originally been

planning for his diversion, but he had enough sense to seize the chance that the kappa had given him. "Help! I can't swim!" he shrieked theatrically, flinging himself backward, thrashing with his arms, and effectively hiding the fact that the water all around him was barely three feet deep.

I dropped back into the shadows under the jetty as voices called and feet pounded overhead. He'd given me my chance; now all I had to do was take it. Quickly I ran and dove, skimming the surface of the shallow water and sinking down deeper as soon as I could.

Long strands of seaweed swept around me, as if I'd dived into a nest of snakes. I pushed through, stroking for the black bulk of the hull ahead of me. My chest tightened with the need to breathe, but I didn't dare come up yet. Even with all of the commotion Jinnai was making, the ship's crew might spot my head breaking the surface.

I caught sight of a single long line that stretched from the ship's stern to the bottom of the harbor—the anchor rope. Grabbing hold of it, I let it guide me to the surface. When I came up for breath at last, I was between the thick anchor line and the stern of the ship, hopefully sheltered from view.

The sailors had gotten a rope down to Jinnai, still in the water. He was clinging to it and loudly calling out his gratitude and blessings on his preservers. Silently I sent my thanks and perhaps a word of apology his way, drew in a second breath, and sank again.

When I opened my eyes under the water, squinting from the sting of the salt, a face was looking directly into mine.

My first thought was that I had encountered a corpse. Her skin was an unhealthy white, with a faint sheen like mother-of-pearl. There seemed to be no end to her long black hair, which swirled around us like the seaweed.

But as she slowly opened both her black eyes and then her wide mouth, I knew she was alive.

She also looked familiar.

I'd seen this face before, in quiet pools, in a cloudy image deep within a brass mirror. This woman adrift in the water looked exactly like me.

"First you," she whispered, her words coming out in a mass of silvery bubbles. She reached toward me with two thin, clawed arms that sprouted at what would have been her shoulders had she been human. "Then him."

I realized with horror that the tendrils and curls of seaweed I had just swum through were not seaweed at all. They were the long, green-black strands of her rippling hair and the coils and curves of her endless body. That body was long enough so that her head would attack me here, while her tail dealt with Jinnai near the shore.

She was a nure onna. A snake-woman.

I pivoted in the water and brought up a foot to kick at her face, while my right hand snatched my knife from its sheath. She looked quite surprised. Perhaps she was accustomed to prey so startled or frightened by her appearance that they didn't muster much of a fight.

Still, she was quick enough to dodge my kick, which was slowed by the weight of the water. Something soft slipped over my ankle and yanked tight. The nure onna laughed, trapping me in a net of bubbles, blinding me even worse than her drifting hair and the sting of the salt.

My left hand, flailing through the water, snatched the anchor line and clung as the pressure around my ankle tried to pull me down.

For a moment my body was taut, my lungs constricting, my throat beginning to ache for air. Grinding my teeth with the effort, I bent the knee of the trapped leg, bringing my ankle up high enough that I could aim a blow with the knife in my right hand, slashing at the loop of the snake's body that held me like a fetter.

The nure onna shrieked as my knife hit its target. The pressure on my ankle loosened, and I shot up so that my head broke the surface. Across the water, I caught a quick glimpse of Jinnai, struggling in earnest now, clinging to his rope but unable to pull himself up. I had no doubt that a loop of the snake-woman's tail held him, the same way she'd tried to hold me.

And she was trying again.

I had a fresh grip on the rope now, and with my lower body still underwater, I kicked and thrashed, trying to fight her off. But it was no use. Tendrils, thin and smooth and muscled, locked around ankles, knees, and waist, and my strength did not match hers. She'd drag me down, smothering me beneath a heavy weight of scaly coils. Salt water would sear my eyes and my throat and my lungs. There was no escape.

Do not waste one moment on a hopeless battle. Don't fight unless you can win.

I let go of the rope and allowed the nure onna to pull me under the water.

I felt the shock of the cold, the swirl of hair, the slippery coils of snake. But for just a moment, the pressure of her coils slackened. I took advantage of that moment to orient myself in the water and, kicking hard, dove straight at her.

When most people are drowning, they struggle mightily for air, fighting for every inch closer to the surface. That must have been what the nure onna was expecting. I'd done the opposite, and she had not been prepared. She flinched as I came through the water, slipping between the curves and loops of her body, both arms out before me, my knife in my hand.

I'd turned myself into a spear, headed straight for the face that looked so much like mine. I heard a howl of pain, and then a fog of bubbles was all around me. Hair as dark as octopus ink swept in. I could not see, but I could feel, and I knew my knife had hit a target. I twisted the blade, drew it back, stabbed again.

Now there was blood in the water, too, smoky clouds of it, twining and spreading.

Was she injured? Was she dead? Was she withdrawing to launch another attack? I could not tell. All around me, the water was choked with snaky coils and drifting hair. Which way should I swim?

I paused, feeling the air inside my lungs tug me up so that I knew where to go. Then I kicked and squirmed and fought my way toward the surface. The snake-woman's body was slack and loose now, but still capable of drowning me if a loop snagged one of my feet.

Something hard rammed into my head—the ship's hull.

I followed it up, breath exploding out of my lungs in a puff like a whale's, loud enough for anyone on the deck to hear me—except that all their attention was concentrated on Jinnai, now hauling himself onto the jetty, and on the coils of snake that were slowly drifting to the surface below him.

Well, I'd wanted a diversion . . .

As quickly as I could, dripping and gasping and shaking wet hair out of my eyes, I climbed the anchor rope, knife gripped between my teeth. I flopped over the railing to lie panting on the deck of the ship.

But I could not stay there. Already I could hear the captain bellowing impatient orders that enough time had been wasted, and hadn't they ever seen a sea snake before, and no, he didn't want to hear superstitious nonsense about bakemono or nure onna and he'd hurl anyone who caused him to miss the tide into the harbor, snakes or no snakes, demons or no demons. Move quickly now!

The captain was as good a diversion as Jinnai had been. While he bellowed I crawled across the deck to a hatch, left open for the last of the cargo, and slithered inside.

I nearly fell down a staircase, so steep it was almost a ladder, and found myself in a room with two straight walls and two curved ones, which I realized must be the hull of the ship. Rolled mats and bundles were lined up along one curved wall, telling me I was in the crew's sleeping quarters.

Each of the straight walls had an open door cut into it. Through the one that led toward the prow of the ship, I could see barrels stacked chest high from wall to wall, with boxes and bundles wrapped in rough, undyed cotton piled on top. That must be where the cargo was stored, and it was where I did not care to be. From the captain's shouts, there was more to be loaded.

It took barely two heartbeats to determine all of this. Before the third, I was running for the other door, the one nearer the ship's stern, as footsteps started down the ladder above my head.

I dove through the door and flattened myself against the wall beside it, where I'd be least likely to be seen. Two sailors came grunting and groaning down the stairs with a heavy bundle slung on a pole between them. I could only hope they'd be too occupied with their burden to spot the wet footprints I'd left behind me.

They didn't notice. I felt every muscle sag slightly with relief as the sailors lugged the cargo toward the hold. Then I let my eyes range over the space where I found myself.

Enough dim light came through the open door for me to see that there was one straight wall, the one at my back. Two curving walls came together in a point opposite me, and along one of them was a rack of polearms, all topped with wicked blades or deadly sharp spikes. Beside them hung grappling irons on long chains. Metal spheres were stacked on shelves, each wrapped in paper and with a length of chain attached. They were called horoku, I knew. A man could grip that chain, swing the sphere over his head, and let go, launching the weapon through the air and onto an enemy's deck. A paper fuse stuck out from each, hinting at the gunpowder and deadly metal shards within.

On the second curved wall was a rack of swords, polished well to flash light into an enemy's eyes. There were enough to arm every sailor on this boat.

My first thought was delight at my luck—I'd found a place where I could rearm myself, replacing the weapons that had been taken from me at Saiko's mansion.

My second thought was that no honest merchant needed this amount of weaponry.

I felt the ship lurch and knew that the captain had gotten his wish. We were under sail at last, and I had stowed away aboard a pirate ship.

EIGHTEEN

Bundles of hay had been lined up alongside the swords, against one of the curved walls of the armory. I'd heard why pirates might need such a thing—a small boat or a raft, stacked with hay and set alight, could be sent toward an enemy ship as a floating bomb.

As far as I was concerned, it was useful for another reason. While the ship made unnerving noises all around me—creaks and groans of wood under strain, sloshing and rushing and slapping of water against the hull—I shifted a few of the bales slightly away from the wall and rearranged some of the hay to make a nest for myself. A few handfuls were also useful to wipe up the wet smears and spots on the floor from my damp feet and dripping clothes.

When I was sure I'd left no trail, I crawled into my shelter and was fairly comfortable, with enough room to stretch out full length and a cushion between my bones and the hard deck. As long as I didn't sneeze, it was a safe hiding place, and I settled in to take stock.

No demons were attacking me at the moment. No ghosts were hovering over me. Perhaps the water all around me had muffled some of the pearl's power, gentled its tendency to disturb and rouse any bakemono it came near. The fox spirit had hinted that it might, and Ichiro had thought so, too. That was to my benefit. And then, I had access to an entire armory. These were my advantages.

Weapons would not be enough, though. I had need of both food and water, and I would have to find a way to get them. If this were a properly planned mission, I'd have a pack full of supplies . . . and, of course, some idea of where I was going.

As I lay, I could feel every movement of the ship ripple through the long, curved pressure of the hull along my back. Being inside a ship, I realized, was not like being inside a house. I'd crept through a warlord's mansion once, in the dead of night, alone and alert to any whisper of noise, any tiny vibration in the bamboo floor or quiver of a paper screen in its frame. I'd felt as if I could sense each living thing under that roof, down to a beetle scuttling across a mat or a dragonfly sleepily flexing its wings.

But here, it felt as if the ship itself were alive, every board singing with tension and speed, every nail tugged to its full length, every line taut and humming like a bowstring at full draw.

It was hard to keep myself from wondering if the ship knew I was here.

Well, if it knew, it did not seem to mind. Perhaps to

the ship, I was just another sailor at rest, or just another rat huddled alone in its hole.

Alone.

I'd achieved what I'd been struggling to do since I'd sat in Shiburo's wineshop. I was alone.

Good. It was better for me, better for my mission, and better for my friends.

They were all safer far away from me, and from this pearl in my pocket. As long as I was its keeper, I could never again ask for help. I should stay as far as I could from anyone I might be tempted to consider a friend.

A ninja has no one.

During my fight with the snake-woman, the briny sea-water must have gotten deeply into my eyes. They stung ferociously, and the inside of my abraded throat ached as well.

I let my eyelids fall shut. The salt of tears would wash away the salt of the sea. In the darkness behind my eyes, I saw blotches of pink and white, like blossoms spangled along the wiry branches of a cherry tree, like Saiko in her gorgeous kimono, standing by herself before a screen that glowed with opulence and beauty.

I felt as if her pale and perfect face were staring at me, and the two of us, together, were bound for who knew where. Of all the people I'd left on the shore, why was it Saiko who haunted me as I drifted into sleep, letting the night of battle and terror and no rest at all claim its due? I'd defeated her for the second time. I'd left her behind in her grand mansion, married to her rich husband, without the one thing she wanted most.

I'd left her alone.

I slept for hours, stirring now and then in my nest of straw to listen to what was happening around me, and then letting my eyes close again. I woke briefly when I felt the motion of the ship begin to change.

The door to my small room had been fastened, so I was in total darkness now. My eyes were useless, but my other senses told me what was happening. Shouts rose and bare feet slapped against the deck as sailors ran back and forth above my head. The pitch of the wind had deepened as well, and the ship leaned into it so that I no longer lay flat. Instead, my body was wedged into the corner made by the wall and the floor.

A storm. There was nothing I could do about that. Either the ship and the sailors would bring us safely through it, or they would not. No actions of mine could help or hinder our survival, so it was best to take no action at all. I slid back into sleep and stayed there, even as the waves heaved the ship higher and higher and then plunged her into troughs that felt deep enough to lead to Ryujin's underwater palace.

It was an entirely new sensation that woke me fully, much later, as if the ship itself had whispered to me, tugging me out of sleep to face a new threat.

The trouble was, I did not know what that threat might be.

I lay still, trying to gather all of the information my senses (minus my sight) could provide. In a moment I realized what change had awakened me.

The ship was not moving.

It no longer leaned into the wind, and the boards no longer quivered with the tug of the sails and the rush of water along the hull. Were we becalmed?

Moving slowly, to keep noise to a minimum, I crawled out of my hiding place and remained crouched by my bales of hay, envisioning the small armory as I'd last seen it, until I was sure I could take a step without tripping over bombs or bringing a rack of polearms crashing down on my head.

Then I rose. My bladder was full and my stomach, in contrast, was so empty it felt as if it had wrapped itself twice around my backbone. Time for a little exploration. Perhaps some foraging as well.

I considered arming myself with some of the weaponry at my disposal, but it was all heavy, crude stuff, for boarding ships or raiding villages—none of it silent or subtle or of much use on a night mission, other than to weigh me down. For now, my knife would do.

Once I reached the door, I knelt and laid my ear against it. I heard no movement and no words from the other side, so I tried to slide the door open.

It was locked.

The latch was simple, though, and easy to lift when I slid the blade of my knife between the door and its frame. Then I could slip out.

The open hatch overhead let in a dim gray light, and I found myself standing in a room full of sleeping men. They lay on their mats in rows along the floor, breathing heavily, snoring thickly. One mumbled in his sleep. Another turned and pushed at a neighbor who'd rolled too close.

Cautiously, I began to pick my way over and around sleeping bodies, placing each foot delicately, probing at the floor with my toes before letting my weight ease down. Stepping on a finger or a shin here could be disastrous.

One man did sleepily curse me as I set my foot down next to his ear. But he didn't open his eyes, and I made it safely to the stairs and crawled up to the deck.

I crouched by the hatch for a moment to let my eyes gather in as much moonlight as possible. A fog was rolling in across the flat sea, giving me added protection.

I noted two masts, one at the bow and one in the center of the boat, with a cabin between them. One sailor leaned against the center mast, but his back was to me. I rose, shook off my furtive crouch, and let myself stride easily across the deck. Figures in the night would all look alike—black and featureless and anonymous. Moving as if I had a right to be there, I'd arouse little suspicion.

I found a deserted stretch of rail near the stern, checked to be sure that no one was in sight, and emptied my bladder over the side. Then I stood retying my belt and considering my next move.

And I was afraid.

It was absurd. Hadn't I fought ghosts and demons? Hadn't I guarded the pearl safely for two years? Hadn't I escaped from Madame Chiyome's clutches not once, but twice? What was there to be frightened of here?

Only space.

The fog hung close to the ship, but it billowed and

shifted like shaken curtains. And through every gap and rent, I could see, or rather sense, the ocean all around me. Once I glimpsed a tiny island, not too far away, between two swags of fog. Other than that, there was only water.

I eased myself down to crouch on the deck and felt a shiver crawl up my spine. One lonely island? That was all? I'd grown up surrounded by green rice fields, ringed by mountains. Then I'd lived two years by the sea, watching ships come and go, learning to judge the time of day by the tides, the weather by the growl of the waves.

But even then, I'd had solid land under my feet. Now that was gone.

Water below, sky above, and this ship like a tiny speck between the two. And me an even tinier speck, clinging to its boards, carried wherever it chose.

Where would this ship take me?

To one of the places marked on Master Ishikawa's map? Or somewhere even more remote and bewildering? And what would I do once I got there? How would I safeguard the pearl? How would I safeguard myself, in a land where I knew nothing?

I craved something solid at my back. When someone climbed out of a hatch and came to join the sailor on watch, handing him a steaming bowl, I seized my chance. As the two men talked in low tones, I slipped behind their backs, moving noiselessly to the cabin. Barrels had been stacked along one side, lashed to pegs to keep them from tumbling about in a storm. I crouched beside them and tried to calm my heart, beating as quickly as a frightened bird's. Tried to steady my breathing.

Fear of the future is foolish. Regret of the past is useless. Attention to the present is survival.

Those old words from an instructor whose name I had never known brought me back to myself. There was no use cowering from empty space, or cringing in fear of what might happen when I had earth under my feet once more. For now, this ship was all I had, and I must turn my senses and my thoughts onto a single question—how could I get from it what I needed? Food, water, and safety?

First, I would watch and listen.

The two sailors finished their conversation, and the one who'd brought the food headed toward the prow and the hatch he had come from. The sailor on watch shifted his weight restlessly. He was not ten yards in front of me now, but there was no reason he should notice me as long as I did not stir. Crouched beside the barrels, I was merely one more black shape among so many others.

The man looked up at the sail, a mat of finely woven reeds. It hung limply. He sighed, settled his shoulders against the mast, and raised the bowl to his lips.

A door in the cabin slid open and bare feet stepped out onto the deck. The sailor set down his bowl and straightened up. "Captain Mori?"

Captain Mori? The same Captain Mori who'd delivered a valuable map to Master Sakuma, one that I had promptly stolen? How surprised he'd be to find his employer's drudge skulking about on the deck of his ship—if, of course, he had looked at her long enough to recognize her again.

"No wind stirring?" the captain asked, still in the doorway of his cabin.

"Not a breath," the sailor answered.

"First that storm out of nowhere," the captain muttered. "Now no wind at all. And what's brought this fog upon us? Get up there and tell me if you can see anything."

The sailor leaped lightly onto the roof of the cabin. The captain took a few steps and turned his head to watch. I seized the opportunity to crawl forward and snatch up the bowl. The warm rice inside was topped by a sliver of fish and a scattering of pickles. I scooped it all into my hand and shoveled it into my mouth, leaving the empty bowl on the deck, then crawled back to my patch of shadow before the sailor could leap down again. Let him think the ship was home to very large and very hungry rats.

"The fog's thickening by the second, Captain," the sailor reported. "I can't see open water on any side. Should we drop anchor?"

"Why? To becalm ourselves more? What has old Ryujin done with our wind?" The captain sounded frustrated and impatient, the voice of a man who scorned to make a fuss over nothing, but who can't shake a sense that things are not as they should be.

No, they are not, little one.

I went still and cold as the voice slid like a blade into my ear.

No, not into my ear. Into my mind.

I put a hand over the pocket where the pearl lay, as if I could silence it.

You think you can take me away from my home? I heard a laugh that made me imagine flame licking up oil. *When I am so close? So close to freedom?*

A deep, hollow drumbeat sounded through the night. Captain Mori jerked in surprise. The drum sounded again, a single, heavy stroke, and now we could hear oars splashing and heaving through the water.

"Wake the men," the captain said grimly. "Get lanterns lit. We need some light." He was turning restlessly, peering over each rail, trying in vain to see something in the darkness except the thick fog that hung in sheets just off the bow, that clung in wisps to the rails and ropes.

The sailor darted down the hatch, calling loudly for the others to wake and arm themselves, and I seized the moment to dash behind the captain's back as he stared out to sea. My current hiding place depended on darkness; if the men lit lanterns, I'd be as visible as a black mushroom in a bowl of rice.

My first choice for concealment would normally be a rooftop, but that would not do here. Sailors look up constantly, to the stars, the clouds, the set of the sails. Crouching low, my hands helping me along, I slipped to the stern and huddled behind the huge winch that raised and lowered the anchor. At my feet lay the anchor itself, a smooth stone as long as I was tall.

All the while, the drum thudded. In time with its beat, oars pulled through the water. Each beat was louder. Each stroke with the oars brought the unknown boat closer.

Pirates must be accustomed to sudden alarms, I thought.

Men were pouring out of the hatchway. Some had strapped on swords; a few had mismatched pieces of armor, perhaps a shoulder guard or a chest protector, which they tied into place with cords. Some swung ropes with grappling hooks or brandished long, spiked poles. Others lugged horoku to pile along the deck or hung lanterns wherever they could. A pale glow illuminated the wooden deck, the black sea, smooth as oil, and the men poised at the railing or perched on the cabin's roof. All were barefoot, half of them stripped to the waist. Every muscle was tense, every eye alert.

A prow cut through the fog, and a ripple of movement passed through the waiting men. His short kimono tightly belted, his two swords swinging, his hair in a samurai's top-knot, Captain Mori strode to the railing to see more clearly what was coming toward his ship.

All eyes were on the intruder now, so I wormed forward for a better view through the railing. These pirates might be adept at fighting off other ships or at ravaging towns and villages, but I doubted that they would be prepared for what they were about to face.

The ship that came out of the fog was much smaller than ours, lower in the water, with no masts for sails. Huddled forms bent over the oars as the drummer in the stern kept up his unwavering beat.

In the prow, a tall, hooded figure stood upright, wrapped in a gray cloak that came down to the ship's deck. Something about his stance said without words that he was the one in command, and it was to him that Captain Mori spoke as the smaller ship drew alongside.

"What do you want?" the captain asked, a hand on the hilt of his longer sword.

The commander of the smaller ship raised his head, his hood falling from a face that was no face at all. Ivory bones, yellowed with age, gleamed in the lantern's light; teeth were bared in a meaningless grin; empty eye sockets held all the shadows of the sea. Around its forehead the thing wore a peaked white headdress, as if it were a corpse prepared by a priest for burial and the journey to the underworld.

But this corpse, it seemed, did not want to make that journey. It opened its fleshless jaw to answer the captain's question.

"You," it said.

Every sailor in every wineshop told stories of creatures like these. A funa-yurei, ghost of a sailor long dead, it was bound to its phantom ship and crew unless it could find a soul to take its place.

This one seemed to think that Captain Mori's would do.

As the captain's sword flashed out and down, a skeletal hand rose to meet it. Mori's blow would have severed any mortal limb, but when the bright blade bit deep into the yurei's bone, it simply closed its bony fingers tight around the steel.

Mori did not have the sense to let go of his blade, and the yurei yanked, pulling him off balance so that he half-fell over the railing. The sailor next to him threw away his grappling iron to fling both arms around his captain's waist. Mori did drop his sword then, but it was too late; the yurei had a solid grip on his right wrist and was steadily pulling him over the side.

One more sailor flung himself on Mori, trying to drag his captain back to safety. Others clustered near the rail, stabbing at the boat with their polearms, trying to force it back. The ghosts at the oars shook back their hoods and reached out with bony hands to snap the poles as easily as I might have snapped a chopstick.

Perhaps half the sailors stood their ground, defending their ship. Others dropped their weapons and fled—but where could they go?

A few climbed the masts, desperate to put as much distance between themselves and the ghosts as they could. One jumped overboard, then another. Were they mad with terror? Or had they decided that an honest death by drowning was better than being dragged aboard a ghost ship?

No, I realized—they were trying to swim to that small island I'd glimpsed through the fog earlier. But they could not reach it. As men swinging horoku lined up at the rail, ready to fling their smoldering bombs onto the yurei's ship, a wave climbed impossibly out of the perfectly calm and flat sea, sweeping toward our ship, tossing swimmers aside as lightly as leaves on the wind. It was the height of our deck when it hit.

NINETEEN

Mori and the men struggling to hold him disappeared under a wall of black water. The funa-yurei's ship rode the wave as easily as a child's toy boat rides a ripple in a stream, but ours lurched to one side. I was swept across the deck in the grip of cold salt water, slammed into a railing, and slid back when the boat tipped the other way. Then I braced myself on hands and knees on the slippery boards, shaking clammy hair out of my eyes, as the water drained away.

Sailors were scrambling to relight the lanterns that the wave had drenched. To my astonishment, Mori was still on board, gripping the rail with his free hand, five of his men now clinging to him. But both his feet were off the deck, and the yurei did not even seem to notice the polearms jabbing at it. It brushed aside a grappling iron swung at its skull and yanked so hard I thought Mori must either go over in the next moment or lose his arm.

More men were bobbing in the water now, and one

was dangerously close to the ghost ship. A yurei dropped its oar to lean over and seize the man's hair. He screamed.

I staggered to my feet and reached inside my jacket to close my hand around the pearl.

Mori would be over the side in a moment. Another wave like that would sink the ship. I'd drown—we'd all drown. Or I'd be dragged aboard that ghost ship to serve for year upon year upon year, until I could snag some poor soul to replace mine.

With one wish, I could stop all of this from happening. But if I wished, I'd have no soul at all.

Laughter bubbled up inside my head, and another wave, not as large, rocked the ship. A sailor, wide-eyed and terrified, slammed into me as he raced by, knocking me off my feet. He dove over the rail, and then—

Silence. I sat up, my ears ringing with the echoes of frantic screams and terrified curses. The fog swept in, thicker than before, prickling my skin with cold, winding clammy fingers down the back of my neck.

Something hit the deck with a thump.

Then the fog swirled away as a fresh breeze filled the sails, and I saw Captain Mori sitting on his deck, blinking in astonishment at the stretch of empty sea before him.

The ghost ship had vanished.

A few men were still bobbing in the water, and those on the ship were throwing ropes or reaching down to them with poles. I got to my feet, drenched and dripping, to scan the dark water in all directions, as far as the light of our lanterns reached.

Nothing but empty ocean.

A heavy hand fell on my shoulder, and a burly sailor twice my weight spun me around to face him. "And who," the man growled, "are you?"

There was not much point in putting up a fight. Even if I could get free, where would I run? Where would I hide? So I let the man haul me across the deck to where Captain Mori was getting to his feet, wringing water from his robes and shaking it from his hair.

"A stowaway?" He looked me over from head to toe, frowning. I could see that he did not recognize me.

"Foul luck, that's what she is," said the man with his fist knotted in my collar. "Or cursed."

Mori studied me, taking in everything from my braid, dripping water over my shoulder, to my bare feet. "She's no ghost herself, at least," he said. "Do we have all of the men back on board?"

"All but Matsuburo. They—those things—they took him." The man holding me shivered. "He didn't deserve a fate like that, Captain."

"No one does." Mori rubbed his wrist, marked where the yurei had gripped him with a livid red ring that would later be a dark bruise. "Speak up, girl. What are you doing on my ship?"

I should have had a lie ready. But my eyes were busy scanning the empty horizon for threats. Where had those ghosts gone? Why had they vanished?

"Lock her in a cargo hold below deck," Mori said impatiently when I did not bother to answer him.

"Captain? But what if she brought this evil on us?"

"She's nothing but a girl, Jiro. What do you suggest, that we fling her overboard?"

The man holding me tightened his grip as if he longed to do just that. And didn't he have a point? I *had* brought this evil on them. I'd put their entire ship in peril. If it hadn't been for me, that poor sailor, Matsuburo, would never have been dragged screaming aboard a ghost ship.

In a way, Jiro was quite right. I *was* cursed. I was a danger, not just to my friends, but to any stranger unfortunate enough to come in my way.

The deck rocked slightly under our feet as the sails bellied out, full of the freshening breeze. "Get her out of my sight. I'll deal with her later," Mori said, and Jiro growled under his breath but swung me around toward the hatch that led belowdecks.

"No. You can't!" I blurted out.

"Oh, now she has a tongue. Can't, did you say?" Mori snorted. "This is my ship, girl. I can do anything I want with you."

I twisted in Jiro's grasp and craned my neck to catch the captain's eyes. "Look out to sea," I told him urgently.

In the light of our lanterns, the water seemed to be boiling. Smooth black bubbles with an oily sheen were rising.

Mori shouted quick orders and crewmen leaped into action, hauling ropes so that the sails snapped tight with the force of the wind. But the ship didn't move. The masts creaked and groaned; the sails strained as if they longed to leap free and fly. Even so, the ship stayed where it was, as if mired in mud.

One sailor somewhere cried out, "Umi-bozu!"

This, I realized with a chill inside me that had little to do with my soaked clothes and the rising wind, was why the funa-yurei had disappeared. They'd abandoned their prey just as a fox will leave its meal to a marauding bear.

The bubbles grew larger by the second. Sailors leaned over the rails to slash at them with boathooks and swing grappling irons at them, but I could see now that the spheres were full of water, rather than air. The weapons passed harmlessly through.

Mori lunged forward to seize my arm. Jiro let go as the captain shook me furiously. "What do you know about this?" he roared. "What kind of a curse have you brought on my ship?"

I didn't know if he could read the guilt on my face, or if he'd simply decided that three strange events—a girl stowaway, a ghost ship, and demons rising from the water—must be connected. It hardly mattered. The umi-bozu were seething and swelling, nearly level with the deck now. In a moment, they would engulf the ship, sailors and all.

"How do we drive them off?" Mori shouted in my face.

"Throw me overboard!" I yelled back at him.

While the captain gaped at me, I seized my own wrist and yanked, pulling against his thumb, the weakest point of the grip, to free my arm from his grasp. Then I ducked low and came up with my shoulder in Jiro's stomach, just below the ribs, knocking him to the deck.

I leaped over his body, sprang to the rail, and dove.

I must have passed straight through the body of at least one umi-bozu, but it felt like nothing but water, heavy and cold, enough of a shock to clench the muscles around my lungs and drive my breath away. I swam hard, striking up for the surface. Somewhere in the distance, in the darkness, there was that small island, the one I'd seen earlier. There was perhaps half a chance—a quarter—a sliver of a hope that I could reach it.

It was more hope than I would have had if I'd stayed on that ship. And perhaps Mori and his poor sailors would survive without me on board. Even pirates didn't deserve to be snatched by ghost sailors or swallowed by umi-bozu.

I seemed to be swimming through endless darkness. Where was the black bulk of the ship's hull, the glimmer of moonlight or lantern light on the water? Would I swim forever and never reach the air?

All around me, huge, round golden eyes blinked open in the murk.

I twisted in the water, tried a different way, but more eyes opened, great gold spheres, like paper lanterns hung in trees at night. They stared hungrily at me, and I remembered that no one knew how umi-bozu killed their prey. They seemed to have no mouths, no teeth, no hands, no claws—just round bodies made of cold seawater and those staring eyes.

How could I defeat these eerie creatures? No weapon could hurt them. No fist or foot could make an impact. I'd been trained for combat; I knew how to fight any opponent. At Madame's school, I'd left instructors twice my size lying in the dirt of the practice yard. But here I was floating, far from solid ground, facing bakemono that could not be injured, let alone killed.

I could do nothing. For the first time since I was younger than Ozu, I was helpless.

Would I be drowned? Devoured?

Then the eyes blinked out, as if the flames inside the lanterns had been snuffed. It seemed that the creatures were gone, melted into the ocean like ink. But I was not relieved.

Something else was tearing through the water toward me. If it could frighten away umi-bozu, what would it do to me?

Moonlight glinted off silver eyes, smaller than those of the umi-bozu. Fangs gleamed; nostrils flared; delicate barbels streamed alongside the creature's head as it swam. A serpentine body, indigo and milky white, longer than Mori's ship, thrashed through the water as a dragon bore down on me.

I felt as if its claws were already sinking into my chest, tightening around my throat as the last of my air bubbled out of my nose. The thing would not have to bite me in two or tear the limbs from my body to kill me. It would just have to keep me underwater half a minute more.

The mouth was opening. If I'd wanted to, I could have dodged between those ivory fangs and swum right down its throat.

A strange slowness seemed to take hold of everything around me, as if I were floating, not just in water, but in time. The dragon's maw gaped, but came no closer. My chest ached, but the pain did not sharpen. And a voice spoke clearly.

You can wish. You can send that writhing snake back to the depths. You can save yourself.

But if I wished, the last tendril of gold around the pearl would melt, and the demon would be free. I'd promised to hold the pearl, to keep it safe. I'd failed a mission only once in my life. I would not do so here. I would not wish.

But if you die, you will also fail, the voice whispered. It bloomed inside my own thoughts. There was no way I could block it out.

Once you drown, the pearl will be cast adrift, the voice insisted. *Anyone could pick it up. Anyone could wish. And someday, surely, someone will.*

There was no hope, then? If I wished, I'd fail. If I died, I'd fail. I could save myself, but not my mission. Not the pearl. No matter what I did, the demon inside the pearl would find its freedom.

This was a battle I could not win. That meant I must not fight it.

I'd said it to Ozu, pulling her off Otani. My instructors at Madame's school had said it to me, over and over again.

Do not waste one moment on a hopeless battle. Don't fight unless you can win.

A samurai might stride boldly into a single combat or lead a doomed charge, sure that although he'd lose his head, he'd win enough glory to compensate. But I was no samurai. I was a ninja. And if I couldn't win one battle, the only choice was to fight a different one.

If I made a wish, the demon would be free. I'd set a hungry, vengeful bakemono loose upon the world. Mori and his sailors would be the creature's first targets, no doubt . . . and who would be next? There was no way to know.

But what if my wish could prevent that? What if my last wish banished the demon back to the underworld?

It would take my soul with it. But my mission would be fulfilled.

I could feel the demon's alarm ring like a bell inside my head. *Don't you dare. Don't*—

Time swept back in around me, and the water dragon lunged.

Claws clamped on my arm. Teeth sank into my shoulder, near the junction with my neck. The snakelike body swirled around me, a whirlpool of blue and white. I had no time to wish or even to think, tumbled and rolled as if in the clutches of a tidal wave, pulled deeper and deeper, away from the air.

Dimly, I was aware of the demon howling as my lungs tightened and tightened, my throat clenched, my mouth opened, and cold salt water rushed in.

TWENTY

I woke in the care of demons.

I didn't realize it at first. For a time I was only conscious of a gentle rocking, a solid surface under my back, and air easing in and out through my aching throat.

This seemed a pleasant enough state to be in, and I was in no hurry to change anything by doing something rash, such as opening my eyes. Sounds drifted over me, strange murmurs and mutterings, and then hands lifted me and tugged at my jacket, trying to ease it off.

This was not good, although I was not sure why. My eyelids were as heavy as though fathoms of water were pressing down on them. Still, with immense effort, I dragged them open.

The warm, yellow light that greeted me was not bright, but it was still intolerable. I squeezed my eyes shut again and blinked over and over, fighting the sting of salt water as well as the dazzle of light.

While I struggled to see, the hands managed to pull my jacket off.

I reached for it, and more hands, gentle enough, caught my arm and held it still. My vision steadied at last, and I saw that someone was bandaging a deep cut just below my collarbone where the dragon's claws or teeth must have scored through my skin.

The thing that was taking such care of my wound was a demon.

It had the shape of a man, but its skin had a ghosly pallor, as if it spent much of its life underground or underwater, far from the touch of the sun. Where it was not that unearthly color, it was spotted and speckled with loathsome brown blobs. Hair sprang from its head in stiff, unnatural curls, the color of fire or rust or sunset. Worst of all were its eyes, a queasy bluish-gray color rather like the flesh of trampled slugs.

Here was an enemy. Something to fight.

But why was an enemy bandaging my wound?

Confusion smothered my first impulse to kick and punch my way free, leaving room only for a shudder of revulsion that worked its way from my bones to my skin. I didn't want this creature touching me.

As I tried to pull away, other hands caught me. These were deep brown, as though their owner had been baked too long in a fire. I turned my head to see a dark demon whose head and face were both smothered in black hair like tightly wound wire, whose teeth showed bright white as it spoke to me in words that made no sense at all.

There were more demons in the background, and they babbled and cawed at me in sounds that could not be called speech. A stench rose from them that clogged my nose, a mix of sweat and stale clothing and long-unwashed bodies and sour breath and rotten meat.

Did other demons smell like this? How had I never noticed before?

My vision blurred again in horror, and my stomach heaved. I struggled, but every muscle was appallingly weak, and pains stabbed my chest with each breath. In this state, I could not have fought off Ozu.

More hands came to hold me down, and the darkest of the demons held a wooden cup against my lips, spilling something cold and bitter into my mouth. I gagged and spat, but still some of it ran down my throat, and slowly the will to fight ebbed from my body.

The pale, speckled demon finished wrapping my shoulder and one of the others picked up my bloody jacket from the floor. He had bronze skin and soft black hair, and so he looked a little more human than the rest.

I focused all my effort on my right arm, which felt as limp as a strand of seaweed, and heaved it up, reaching out to him. My jacket . . . I needed it. Straining, I managed to snag the sleeve in my fingers.

The thoughts inside my head seemed to be muffled in soft, fuzzy cotton. Still, I knew there was something about my jacket, something important. But the bronze-skinned demon smiled at me and patted my hand, and my fingers slipped from their hold on the wet cloth.

It was too hard to keep fighting. I'd been doing it for so long. I'd defeated or outwitted every enemy in my path. I'd faced down demons and ghosts and friends. Of course, I knew I should be running, shouting, wrestling, kicking, freeing myself from these hideous creatures and their plans for me. But I was tired now, so tired it hurt to think. No one could fight forever.

I gave up the jacket and whatever was so important about it. Let him take it. It was his now. All I wanted was sleep.

My eyes closed, shutting out the sight of the demons. Their inhuman sounds swirled around me and melted away.

* * *

After some time, I felt my jacket, still damp and stiff with salt, being wrapped around me once more. Someone picked me up. I turned my head drowsily from the feel of rough cloth under my cheek. A fresh, damp breeze touched my face. The rocking grew stronger. Small waves slapped on wood. Oars swept through water. But everything was dark, as if my eyes had been glued shut with cobwebs.

I could not give up, though. Not now.

There was something I needed to do. A mission. I had a mission, and I could not complete it flat on my back with my eyes closed.

I could not rest. Could not sleep. Could not let the peaceful darkness keep me.

With a huge effort, I wrenched myself awake, to find that the demons had vanished. Had they flown off on the wind, dived beneath the sea, melted into the air? I could not guess. But they were gone, and I was lying in a hut next to a smoky driftwood fire. A wrinkled old woman knelt beside me, peering into my face. She jumped back when my eyes struggled open.

She was, I learned after we'd both gotten over our moment of surprise, the mother of the fisherman who owned the hut. She was kind enough to me, as were her son and his wife. They gave me the freshest fish and the softest sleeping mat and the warmest spot by the fire. They leaped to bring me anything I might want before I had time to ask. But they were clearly wary of me, which was only natural, since I'd been brought to their door by a boatload of demons.

They told me how the demons had rowed ashore, wearing the most outlandish clothing, babbling like animals and stinking like garbage. One, speckled and pale as a fish's belly, and another, dark as burnt rice, had handed me over. Others had filled up barrels of water at a nearby spring and, with gestures and more of their squawking attempts at words, indicated a desire for half my host's store of dried and salted fish.

They'd offered in exchange a few outlandish coins which, the fisherman said, did not even have a hole in the center. When the man would not accept them or anything else in trade, the demons had gabbled a bit among themselves and then taken their fish and their departure, rowing off toward an enormous ship like a floating castle anchored not far offshore. They'd left several of the strange coins on a rock by the waterside. No member of the family had been brave enough to touch them, and the tide had washed the little golden heap away.

I'd slept a day and a half before finally hauling myself awake.

It was clear to the fisherman's family that they were supposed to care for me. It was clear to me that they would be happy when I was gone.

But I couldn't concern myself too deeply about their fears, or about the baffling behavior of the demons. In all my encounters with bakemono, I had not met any who bargained for fish. Or who were merely and simply kind.

I barely wondered at it, however. I did not have the heart.

When I'd opened my eyes to find the fisherman's old mother peering anxiously at me, I'd sat up and instantly clapped a hand to the pocket inside my jacket, then frantically torn the ties loose and pulled the pocket itself inside out.

It was empty. The pearl was gone.

Had it been washed out in the water? Had the dragon snatched it? Had the demons stolen it? It didn't matter. It was gone, and that meant I'd failed.

Whenever I died—and that might be soon, considering the number of enemies I'd managed to accumulate—the demon I'd carried in my pocket for two years would be set loose. I'd had a chance to banish it back to the underworld, but I'd been slow, and stupid, and weak, and now that chance was gone.

I'd been handed a mission by the gods themselves, and

I had not been able to get it done.

I spent that first day curled up by the fire, staring into the black coals at the heart of the flames, feeling nothing but the dull, deep ache of failure. On the second day I drank a cup of salty soup so that the fisherman's wife and mother would stop offering me the bowl, taking turns to creep near and then retreat anxiously when I looked up or waved them away.

It was irritating.

At last I snatched the bowl from the wife's hand and gulped the soup down. And suddenly the little hut, its single room smoky from the damp fire in its center, fishing spears leaning in a corner, nets strung from the rafters, was chokingly small and smelly. It was also insufferably crowded, even if there were only two people in it apart from myself. Both women, huddled together, watched wordlessly as I surged to my feet, wincing from the ache in my bandaged shoulder. I pushed my way outside.

Their hut stood by itself on a stony stretch of beach, scooped in a curved bay as if the sea had taken a hungry bite out of the land. The boards of the little building had weathered gray under the rain and the salt winds. The stones were gray. The clouds overhead were gray. The sea heaved and rumbled as shallow gray waves spat dirty white froth against the shore.

Not too far from my feet, I spotted something round and flat and not-gray, wedged half under a rock. I bent to pick it up. It was one of the demon's gold coins.

On one side was a design of two crossed lines, on the

other a shape like a shield. I straightened, rubbing my thumb over the cold, slick, wet metal, pondering the oddity of demons who carried coins, who tried to pay for what they took, and who'd picked up a drowning girl from the waves.

Then a flash of white caught my eye.

Where the bay ended, a grassy slope rose to a little headland. The fox was sitting there with her brushy tail tucked neatly against her feet, waiting for me.

I'd been a failure, but that did not mean I had to be a coward, too. I set my teeth and trudged across the smooth, shifting, treacherous stones until I reached the headland, climbing up to kneel before the fox.

I bowed.

"I am sorry," I said into the short, wiry grass beneath my face. "I failed."

I wouldn't add more, anything weak or sniveling like *I tried* or *I did my best*. Trying did not matter. Only the mission mattered. And the mission had not been fulfilled.

Gentle fingers touched my shoulder, and when I looked up, a beautiful woman in a snow-white kimono knelt before me.

Her eyes held pity. I did not want pity. I wanted myself back, the self who had never failed a mission, not since I was sent to murder Ichiro and rescued him instead.

I wanted to be the Kata who had stolen every jewel and coin and scrap of information Master Ishikawa ever wanted. Who had won every bout in the practice yard. And she was gone. I could never be that girl again.

"Kata, no," the fox-woman said.

Her deep voice was warm as fur, rich as earth.

"You did not fail," she told me.

"The dragon," I protested, my tongue clumsy with shock. "It took the pearl—or I lost it—or—"

"The dragon came to help you," she said gently. "I told you you'd find new allies in the sea, did I not? As loyal as those you found on land. The dragon saved you."

Saved me? It had cut my shoulder open and hauled me through the water until I nearly drowned. If it hadn't been for the dragon—

If it hadn't been for the dragon, the umi-bozu might have devoured me. If it hadn't been for the dragon, I might have wished on the pearl one last time.

The woman in the white kimono nodded when she saw I was beginning to understand. "After it kept you from spending the pearl's last wish, the dragon brought both you and the pearl where it knew a ship had been blown far enough off course to find you," she told me.

I remembered the storm that had shaken Mori's ship. Had it also brought the demons' vessel close to this shore?

"On that ship, you did what you were meant to do," the fox-woman went on. "You gave the pearl to its next guardian."

I *gave* the pearl? But it had been mine. I did not—I would never—

My fingers touched the empty pocket of my jacket, the cloth still stiff with salt and dried blood.

The black-haired demon had picked up my jacket from the deck. I'd struggled to seize hold of it, but at last I'd given in. *Let him take it,* I'd thought. I'd handed over the jacket, with the bloody pearl inside it.

After fighting for two years to keep the pearl safe, I'd given it to a demon.

"And that guardian will complete the mission you were sent on," the fox-woman said, speaking clearly over the new and sickening swirl of failure and guilt inside my head. "He will take the pearl far from these shores. At such a distance, the demon's power will wither until nothing remains. It will never grant another wish, and so it will never be freed. Oh, I see company has arrived."

As I sat back on my heels, too stupefied to be happy or even relieved, she glanced up at the sky. I followed her gaze and saw a great flock of dark wings overhead, all swirling together like a single scrap of black silk caught in a gale. They might have been crows, but I believed they were not.

"I asked them to act as guides," the fox-woman said. "They've brought someone you may like to see."

When I looked back down from the sky, the fox was loping away, a spot of white that soon merged into the gray and windswept landscape.

The tengu wheeled above my head and up into the sky again, cawing their raucous laughter, and at the end of the beach where the fox had disappeared, I glimpsed a familiar lean figure.

Jinnai stumbled and slid over the loose stones along the shore, climbed the headland, and collapsed into a heap beside me.

"Following you does lead me into the most desolate

places," he said, looking with distaste at the lonely shore and the humble hut.

"Why do you do it, then?" I asked, but I couldn't find any exasperation to lace into my tone. I had not failed after all. My mission was over. The pearl was gone but safe, out of my hands, out of this land.

"I told you. I'm in love with you. Despite the fact that, apparently, you don't listen to a word I say. So are there ghosts here who are about to attack us, or giant snakes in the water, or anything else I should know about?"

I cast a glance at the tengu, vanishing now into the cloudy sky. "No. I don't think I'll see many bakemono from now on." But I'd always know they were there, filling every shadow. I'd always know that the world was stranger, more dangerous, and more astonishing than most people would ever believe.

"Excellent!" Jinnai's grin was wide. "So all we have to worry about is the fact that Master Ishikawa will be hunting you down? I did warn you that it was a bad idea to steal from him. And, of course, that the entire Takeda family would be delighted to have your head? Possibly mine as well?"

I thought for a moment. "I think that's all."

"Marvelous. Nothing we can't handle between us." Jinnai sighed with what looked like genuine satisfaction. "That is . . ."

He glanced at me and then away, and I saw something remarkable in his eyes. Was it uncertainty?

"Those flying friends of yours were quite insistent that

I come with them," he said, keeping his gaze on the restless water. "It's not exactly easy to refuse." That was certainly true. If an entire flock of tengu wanted me to go somewhere, I knew that I'd have little choice.

"But I don't have to stay. I know you never . . ." His voice trailed off. My brain, dulled by exhaustion and the degradation of failure and then the astonishment of relief, began to stir slowly to life.

Not just uncertainly from Jinnai, but humility as well? That was certainly new.

"If you tell me to, I'll go," he said simply. He did not turn his face away from the sea.

He was offering me what I thought I'd wanted since the night I'd dragged him out of a bush. It would be simple enough to take it.

All my life, I'd been taught to trust no friend, rely on no ally. It was my failure to follow that training, surely, that had put myself, my friends, and my mission in peril.

And yet—what had the fox spirit said? That the water dragon had been as loyal an ally as those I'd found on the land?

To my surprise a memory flickered inside my head. When I'd been Saiko's prisoner, Madame had studied the two of us, as if she were deciding who would win.

But she hadn't merely looked at me and Saiko. Her gaze had moved to the others as well. My allies. My friends. Madame had weighed them in the balance, too. And then she'd made her choice.

All I'd been able to see was the ways my allies had

imperiled my mission. I'd been blind to the ways they had saved it.

Without the water dragon, I would have sacrificed my soul when I spent the pearl's last wish.

Without Yuki, I'd have been lost in a forest that never ended, or inside thoughts that would not let me go.

Without Jinnai, the pearl would likely be in Saiko's hands this moment.

Without Masako and Tomiko, I'd have stayed in a cage. Oh, I could have wished myself out—but if I had, I'd have been trapped inland, miles from the sea, with the demon of the pearl calling on every bakemono between me and the water to block me from my destination.

If I were faithful to my old training, I'd leave this beach now, alone. I'd find my way to a new city—the capital, perhaps—where my skills would earn a living. I'd walk off into the world by myself, as Tomiko had done. I'd live for my own advancement, as Saiko always would.

But if I'd been faithful to my old training, my mission would have failed. Instead, it had succeeded. I was free.

Free to decide what I would do. Free to decide whom I might trust, even if the person I chose to trust was a thief and a liar.

Free to believe, perhaps, what this thief and liar had once said—that he had never lied to me. Not even when he claimed to love me.

Which didn't mean that I had to love him in return. But it did mean that it might not be ridiculous to consider it.

I cleared my throat.

"I suppose," I said, and heard uncertainty in my own tone. Perhaps even humility.

"If you want to . . . ," I went on. "You can . . ." I paused to cough. "Come with me."

Jinnai's entire body twitched. He sat straighter, turning to me, the surprise on his face melting into delight.

I scowled at him. I'd made no promises. All I'd said was that he didn't have to go away.

But before I could remind him of this, he took my hand.

My eyes dropped to his fingers. Deft, and warm, and very gentle, they brushed across the bandage he'd wrapped around my palm, so firmly and so well that it had stayed in place through all my underwater battles, my days and nights of despair.

Under the gray sky, with the last echoes of the tengu floating away, and the fisherman's boat making toward land, hauling what would turn out to be (he told us later) the biggest catch of his lifetime, Jinnai met my scowl with a half-smile.

"Where should we go first?" he asked, and then he answered himself. "Wherever we want. You're the deadliest flower I know. I'm the best thief there is. And there's always more treasure to steal."

Author's Note

Ninjas

Ninjas did not leave many records behind them. They worked in secret, after all, and a ninja who ended up in the history books probably didn't do a very good job. However, we do know that ninjas (who also called themselves *shinobi* [shih-NOH-bee]) played an important role in the feudal age of Japan, and that they handled such jobs as espionage and assassination, things that the bold warrior class, the samurai, would have considered beneath them.

It can't be proven that there were female ninjas, but some may have existed. There are certainly stories and legends that speak of *kunoichi* (KOO-noh-EE-chee) or "deadly flowers." One such story tells of Mochizuki Chiyome (or Chiyojo), who is said to have taken in girls orphaned or abandoned in the civil wars that spread through Japan in the 1500s, and then trained these girls as spies and information gatherers—in a word, as ninjas.

For more information on female ninjas and Madame Chiyome, you might enjoy:

Shadow Warrior by Tanya Lloyd Kyi

Uppity Women of Medieval Times by Vicki León

Ninja: The True Story of Japan's Secret Warrior Cult by Stephen Turnbull

Ninja Attack! True Tales of Assassins, Samurai, and Outlaws by Hiroko Yoda and Matt Alt

Ghosts and Demons

Japanese folklore tells of ghosts (*yurei*) and other supernatural creatures, called *yokai* or by an old name, *bakemono*. Some *bakemono* are merely mischievous or spooky but harmless. A few are even helpful. But beware—others are terrifying.

Double-tailed cat or *neko-mata* (NEH-ko MAH-tuh): Some say that once a cat reaches a certain age, its tail will split in two. It is then a *neko-mata*. These double-tailed cats can speak, sing, and dance, but they take part in more sinister pursuits as well. They crave human flesh. They can also raise corpses from the dead to do their bidding.

Fox: The Japanese red fox, or *kitsune* (KEY-tsoo-nay), is a clever trickster, and some are able to transform themselves into human beings (although they tend to keep the tail). They are powerful and unpredictable creatures. Some may play tricks on human beings, some may kill, and some may be helpers or guides. White foxes are messengers of Inari, the god of rice, wealth, and the harvest.

Iron-toothed rat or *tesso* (TEH-so): An oversized rat with teeth made of metal, the *tesso* can control smaller, lesser rats. It normally creeps into temples and libraries and chews sacred texts and scrolls to bits. Perhaps its followers have more mundane appetites, and so attacked Kata and her companions.

***Kappa* (KAH-pah):** With a shell like a turtle's on its back, the *kappa* lurks in shallow waters, waiting to ambush and drown unwary travelers. They sometimes challenge victims to a wrestling match. If you are ever challenged by a *kappa*, remember to speak to it respectfully and bow. It will bow back, and water will drain from the small depression on its head. This will render it powerless.

***Moku-moku ren* (MOH-koo MOH-koo ren):** These animated eyes may appear on the rice paper panels of old and damaged screens. Though startling, they are not dangerous.

***Nurikabe* (NOO-ree-KAH-bay):** A sort of invisible, living wall that may spring up to block your path. If you find yourself inconvenienced by a *nurikabe*, the secret is to run a staff or a stick along its base, where it meets the ground. This will cause it to vanish.

Sea of Trees, or *Jukai* (joo-KIE): The unofficial name for an area of wilderness at the foot of Mount Fuji. It's easy to become lost in this dense forest, and compasses are said to malfunction there. But this alone can't explain why so many travelers to the Sea of Trees never return. Sadly, the *Jukai* is known throughout Japan as a place where people commit suicide. No one knows why this particular place is the site of so many tragedies. Maybe Kata and her companions came across a similar eerie place when they entered the copse of trees that had power over their thoughts and fears.

Ship ghosts or *funa-yurei* (FOO-nuh YOO-ray): The spirits of those who have drowned at sea are known to band together and do their best to sink boats with living passengers. Some tales suggest that a *funa-yurei* cannot rest unless it finds another soul to take its place.

Snake-woman or *nure onna* (NEW-ray OHN-nah): With the body of an enormous snake and the head of a woman, the *nure onna* lurks in shallow waters, ready to attack swimmers and devour them. Sometimes she floats at the surface with only her human face showing and calls for help, as if she is drowning. Anyone approaching to assist her will soon regret the kindness.

***Umi-bozu* (OO-mee BOH-zoo):** These monsters lurk in deep ocean waters and arise from the depths to engulf ships and sailors. Their smooth heads and glowing eyes seem to be formed out of water, and they are almost impossible to injure or kill.

Water dragon: Perhaps the greatest dragon in Japanese folklore is Ryujin, the fierce god who dwells in an undersea palace and controls the rising and falling of the tides. All snakes are his messengers. Perhaps it was Ryujin himself, or one of his servants, whom Kata encountered in the ocean off Japan.

If you are interested in knowing more about Japanese yokai, you might try *Yokai Attack! The Japanese Monster Survival Guide* and *Yurei Attack! The Japanese Ghost Survival Guide*, both by Hiroko Yoda and Matt Alt.

Pirates

In the sixteenth century, the people of Japan were known for their skills in seafaring (and also in swimming). Not all of them used these skills for lawful purposes. "Wa" is an old name for inhabitants of Japan, and sea raiders in Asia were commonly called wako, meaning "pirates from Japan," even if their crews included members from many nations.

Some pirates were ragtag bands who found places to hide on the smaller Japanese islands. Others were warlords or openly employed by them. They raided coastal villages and towns in Japan itself and the nearby countries of China and Korea (then called Choson), terrifying inhabitants and carrying off rice, gold, silver, and slaves.

If you would like to know more about Japanese pirates, you might read *Fighting Ships of the Far East, volume 2: Korea AD 612–1639* and *Pirate of the Far East: 811–1639*, both by Stephen Turnbull.

Don't miss Kata's other adventure:

DEADLY FLOWERS

I was sparring in the practice yard the day the new girl arrived.

Weak. She looked weak, and frail, and modest, and beautiful, and shocked at what she was seeing. . . .

I stood there, barefoot, my hair spilling out of its braid, in my undyed, ragged jacket and trousers, covered in dust and straw and with a bit of blood trickling from my nose, and thought, She won't last a week.

Kata has been training to be a deadly flower—a female ninja—nearly her entire life. She knows the rules that a ninja must live by better than she knows her own heart.

Secrecy is your armor. Betray your thoughts to no one. Trust no friend. Trust no ally.

She's more than ready for her first mission . . . until she learns that it's to be an assassin. Even then, she's sure that she'll be successful. After all, she knows more ways to kill than she can count.

But when Kata discovers that her target is just a young boy and that her new accomplice is his slightly older sister, suddenly her mission becomes much more complicated than she bargained for. Faced with taking someone's life or confronting the dire consequences of failure in her mission, Kata must make a difficult choice, one that leads her into a more dangerous battle than she ever expected.

Praise for DEADLY FLOWERS

★"This action-packed book will captivate both girls and boys."
—*School Library Connection*, starred review

"Genuinely thrilling, with surprises at every turn and a solid emotional core, this is just the thing for Percy Jackson fanatics thirsty for more, more, more." —*Booklist*

"Ninja-loving readers will rejoice at this clever, dangerous, vivacious book." —*Bulletin of the Center for Children's Books*

"In Kata and Saiko, Thomson has created heroines who are opposites yet manage to use their strengths to take control of their lives under the social restraints of their time. . . . Edge-of-your-seat action." —*Kirkus Reviews*